"So, what   *you have*

Jason smiled. "What, you can't read my mind?"

"Oh, so you want to play? Reading minds isn't really one of my talents, but I'm willing to give it a try if you're willing to chance it."

Desire lit up his eyes. Jason took a step forward, the warrior in him not afraid of the dare in her posture.

Skin touched skin. And pow. Cherry felt his heat, his muscles coil as he braced his body, then the scent of him. Her lips against his cheek, the softness of skin, the harshness of bristles.

The reality of love.

Her system absorbed the shock even as her mind opened and her senses flared. Cherry knew, just knew, in that moment that this man, this near stranger, was her soul mate.

Fear and denial rose up fast and hard.

Oh, no. No. No! She turned and ran, not caring who saw or what impression she left behind her. She was running for her life.

Dear Reader,

Working with talented writers is one of the most rewarding aspects of my job. And I'm especially pleased with this month's lineup because these four authors capture the essence of Silhouette Romance. In their skillful hands, you'll literally feel as if you're riding a roller coaster as you experience all the trials and tribulations of true love.

Start off your adventure with Judy Christenberry's *The Texan's Reluctant Bride* (#1778). Part of the author's new LONE STAR BRIDES miniseries, a career woman discovers what she's been missing when Mr. Wrong starts looking an awful lot like Mr. Right. Patricia Thayer continues her LOVE AT THE GOODTIME CAFÉ with *Familiar Adversaries* (#1779). In this reunion romance, the hero and heroine come from feuding families, but they're about to find out there really is just a thin line separating hate from love! Stop by the BLOSSOM COUNTY FAIR this month for Teresa Carpenter's *Flirting with Fireworks* (#1780). Just don't get burned by the sparks that fly when a fortune-teller's love transforms a single dad. Finally, Shirley Jump rounds out the month with *The Marine's Kiss* (#1781). When a marine wounded in Afghanistan returns home, he winds up helping a schoolteacher restore order to her classroom...but finds her wreaking havoc to his heart!

And be sure to watch for more great romances next month when Judy Christenberry and Susan Meier continue their miniseries.

Happy reading,

Ann Leslie Tuttle
Associate Senior Editor

Please address questions and book requests to:
Silhouette Reader Service
U.S.: 3010 Walden Ave., P.O. Box 1325, Buffalo, NY 14269
Canadian: P.O. Box 609, Fort Erie, Ont. L2A 5X3

Flirting
with
Fireworks

TERESA
CARPENTER

Blossom County
Fair

SILHOUETTE *Romance*®

Published by Silhouette Books

America's Publisher of Contemporary Romance

To Chris, Judy and Jill. Thanks for sharing my vision.

To Mom and Bud, for supporting my dream
from the very beginning.

And to the Wednesday night critique group, including
Terry Blain who answered my last-minute call for help.
You ladies are the greatest.

 SILHOUETTE BOOKS

ISBN 0-373-19780-2

FLIRTING WITH FIREWORKS

Copyright © 2005 by Teresa Carpenter

Books by Teresa Carpenter

Silhouette Romance

Daddy's Little Memento #1716
Flirting with Fireworks #1780

Silhouette Special Edition

The Baby Due Date #1260

TERESA CARPENTER

is a fifth-generation Californian who currently lives amid the chaos of her family in San Diego. She loves living there because she can travel for thirty minutes and be either in the mountains or at the beach. She began her love affair with romances in the seventh grade when she talked her mother into buying her a category romance; she and romance have been together ever since.

Teresa has worked in the banking and mortgage industry for fifteen years. When not working or writing, she likes to spend time with her nieces and nephew, go to the movies and read. A member of RWA/San Diego, she has participated on the chapter board in numerous positions, including president, VP Programs, newsletter editor and conference coordinator. She is especially proud of having received the chapter's prestigious Barbara Faith award.

THE BLOSSOM BEE

The Buzz About Town
by Harriet Hearsay

The carnies are coming! The carnies are coming!

Have you chosen your side in the biggest controversy to hit Blossom since the feud over whose mutt impregnated Minnie Dressler's miniature poodle, Poopsie? Mayor Jason Strong has confirmed the carnival will be in the fair this year. But don't you know the good mayor wants no chance of a repeat of the Swindle? So if you're wanting to know if there's a love interest coming into your life, flip to the astrology page, because there will be no fortune-teller at the fair this year!

Prologue

Cherry Cooper leaned into the curve, taking it low and tight. Hot wind whipped past her as she opened her cycle up on the straightaway and throttled down. She loved the power and speed, loved that both were under her control.

She savored the moment in a world suddenly out of sync. Especially as every mile under her tires brought her closer to Blossom City, Texas.

A sense of unease caused her to slow down as she approached the outskirts of the city. Being psychic, Cherry paid attention to her senses.

She looked inward to determine if the feeling had to do with the city or her emotions in eventually losing her grandmother to this place.

Crossing the city limits marker, she had her answer.

A gray pall loomed over the city, a sense of sadness, as if the spirit of the city suffered from a festering wound.

More than that, bad times were coming to town.

Not a good omen since in little more than a month she'd be part of a carnival troupe coming into town for a four-week-long stint at the county fair. Cherry believed in omens.

She concentrated on the feeling, but it remained vague, out of reach. Which meant the trouble would touch her life.

Great. More trouble to deal with.

She already had her grandmother's health to worry over. Nona suffered from arthritis and recovery from her recent hip surgery had been slow and plagued with complications. Her traveling days were definitely over. She'd chosen Blossom City as the place she wanted to settle.

All Cherry knew about Blossom City was that her mother had died here. Cherry had been five days old when her grandmother bundled her up and took her on the road. It had been just the two of them ever since.

Whatever it took, Cherry would find a home for Nona. Her grandmother had dedicated her life to taking care of Cherry. Now it was her turn to take care of Nona.

With another surgery scheduled for the end of the week, in Lubbock, Texas, Cherry wanted to take her grandmother something positive to focus on. Something to represent her potential home in Blossom City—flyers, the classifieds, whatever she found.

Cherry added another goal to her list: to see if the city was worthy of Nona.

Cherry followed the signs to City Hall, right to the heart of the city. The bank and professional offices, along with the city and county buildings, ringed City Hall Park, an oasis of grass, flowers and a romantic gazebo. A beauty parlor, a dress shop, a hardware store and The BeeHive Diner were also in view.

Here the pall shifted, lifted. Goodness and joy pushed the heaviness away. The promise of a good life bloomed here, along with the purple pansies, yellow roses and pretty daisies.

For the first time since entering the city limits, Cherry smiled. Yes, Nona could happily live here.

Yes, this city had suffered, but it was regrouping and regrowing. She had the sudden clear image of a stronger, more united Blossom City.

But that was the future.

Chapter One

One month later

Jason Strong followed a Harley Sportster into City Hall's parking lot. He spared a thought for the biker's business and hoped he was only passing through town.

With the fair coming to town early next week, the last thing Jason needed was to worry about a biker invasion as well. Of course, there could be an upside. If the Committee for Moral Behavior caught sight of the slim figure in black leather, the biker might distract committee members from their objections to the carnival troupe arriving soon.

Jason grabbed his briefcase and climbed from his car. The biker set the bike stands, then swung a long, leather-clad leg over the seat to stand next to the Harley. Struck by the way the biker moved, by the lithe grace and slight stature, Jason wasn't really surprised when the helmet came off to reveal a head of dark brown, corkscrew curls and a delicate profile.

Taking in the willowy figure, the in-your-face leather, the hint of red in the wild curls, he had the sinking feeling his peaceful existence teetered on a fault line. A fear that was confirmed when the exotic stranger turned and nailed him with eyes black as the leather covering her every curve. The impact of her perusal ran like a hand over his body until she broke contact to speak to a woman entering the building.

He let out a hissing breath. No doubt about it. Trouble had come to town on a Harley.

Hopefully she wouldn't be staying long.

Life had fallen into a predictable pattern for Jason. Just how he wanted it. His daughter, his family, his town were all happy and healthy.

For the most part.

Okay, so his daughter was growing up without her mother, his mother was running away from her responsibilities and the town was still recuperating from economical shock. The point was, they were all doing fine. And, with time, would do better.

With that comforting thought, he turned his back on the tempting vision in black and headed for the familiar ground of his office.

Ten minutes later, his secretary buzzed him, "Jason, do you have a few minutes for Lady Pandora?"

Lady Pandora? He nearly groaned aloud. This was worse than he thought. What were the chances of two exotic strangers visiting City Hall today?

"Send her in."

He rose from behind his mahogany desk as his secretary escorted the leather-clad Lady Pandora into his office.

She was more beautiful than he'd at first thought. Dark curls framed delicate features highlighted by high cheekbones, barely arched brows and shiny pink, lushly full lips. Up close, he corrected his previous assumption. Her eyes weren't black; they were a decadent dark chocolate. And they snapped with challenge.

"Ms. Pandora." He held out his hand and received her gloved one in response.

She returned his firm grip briefly before taking a step back and gracefully sinking into one of the chairs fronting his desk. She peeled off her gloves and pulled the zipper down on her jacket revealing black lace underneath.

He resumed his seat, surreptitiously wiping the sweat from his palms. "What can I do for you?"

"You can allow me my rightful place in the fair," she stated in clear terms, her voice soft yet assertive.

"What place might that be?" As if he couldn't guess. Lady Pandora, right. More like Lady Charlatan. Jason scowled, disappointed that this lovely, exotic creature was most likely a parasite of the worst kind. She had to be the fortune-teller he'd banned from this year's fair.

In his experience, fortune-tellers were frauds who preyed on the innocent and unsuspecting, dealing out false hope and bad advice. And that's when they weren't outright cheating the gullible public out of hard-earned savings.

"I'm sure you're aware the city has chosen not to have a fortune-teller at the fair this year, Ms. Pandora."

"Call me Ms. Cooper. Lady Pandora is my professional name. As you've guessed, I'm a teller of fortunes. You disapprove, though I believe you judge us too harshly. There are the unscrupulous in every vocation, that doesn't mean all are frauds and parasites." Her brown eyes met his; hers were rounded in exaggerated innocence. "It may surprise you to learn, Mr. Mayor, that politicians are often thought to lack integrity and to have only their own interests at heart, taking advantage of the masses while lining their own pockets."

Jason frowned, taking the hit directly to the gut. She'd pushed one of his hot buttons square on the head. Neither did he miss the fact that her choice of words so closely echoed his thoughts. He shook off the unease the coincidence generated. He didn't believe in mind readers, in being able to see into the future. If she expected him to change his mind, either about his beliefs or about letting her into the fair, then she obviously wasn't very good at her job.

"Ms. Cooper, I'm afraid you've wasted your time. Blossom has a bad history with fortune-tellers, which is why the ban stands."

"I'm sorry to hear that, because I'm ready, willing and able to perform at this fair. I'm contracted with this carnival troupe, which means I can't go to another fair and even if I could, it's too late at this delayed date."

She spoke softly, slowly, the cadence so serene that the words lulled and suggested on an elemental level. Jason caught himself leaning forward to catch every word. Disgusted, he shook off her seductive spell.

"I sympathize, but that's hardly my problem."

"It is, actually. I'd happily trot along my merry way, but I need the income from this fair. Not just for myself, but for my family. And your ban is not only insulting, you're frustrating my purpose."

He frowned at her use of the legal terms: ready, willing and able, frustrated purpose. Her message came through loud and clear. Ms. Cooper had obviously been talking to a lawyer.

He might be worried except he'd drawn up the contract and knew it was airtight. Which didn't mean she couldn't contest it if she had the time, money and inclination. Given her transient lifestyle, he doubted she'd go to the effort. Admiring the cling of leather to soft curves, he almost regretted the necessity of sending her away. But the last thing Blossom—or he—needed was the trouble she represented.

"Still not my problem, Ms. Cooper. We contracted with the carnival months ago. I made it clear at the time no fortune-teller would be allowed in the fair.

You need to take your grievance up with the carnival troupe."

"Oh," she waved a slim-fingered hand, uncrossed impossibly long legs and flowed lithely to her feet. "I have a better idea."

She inclined her head as if she'd heard something interesting, then focused those brown, brown eyes on him. "So you're an attorney as well as the mayor. How fortunate the townspeople of Blossom have you to safeguard their interests. But you needn't worry, they have nothing to fear from me."

She smiled a serene smile that did nothing to calm him and everything to arouse his suspicions, distracting him so he almost missed her next statement. "I believe we'll let them decide whether I should be allowed in the fair."

He shot to his feet and met her at the door. The scents of leather and honeysuckle made an intoxicating mix, making him light-headed until he pulled himself together.

Just when had he developed such a biker babe fixation? The sooner this hot mix of trouble vacated his town, the better.

"There's nothing to decide, Lady Pandora. I regret there's no place for you in Blossom."

She sauntered through the doorway, hips swaying provocatively before turning to deliver the last word. "Oh, no need for regret." This time her smile was pure challenge. "An apology at the end of the fair will do. You don't have a problem admitting when you're wrong do you, Your Honor?" She snapped to attention and offered a mock salute. "Or should I say, General, sir?"

"What?" Shock rocked him back on his heels. How could she possibly know his childhood nickname? His grandfather had called Jason Little General when he was a tiny kid.

"The contract may not be as airtight as you think." She taunted him. "You were distracted remember? Someone didn't feel well."

Rikki. His daughter had had the flu. How could Lady Pandora know that? Before he pulled himself together enough to ask, she escaped out the door.

He stabbed his secretary's call button.

"Yes, sir?"

"Get me Sheriff McCabe on the line. I want to know everything there is to know about Lady Pandora."

"Oh, wasn't she just wonderful, Jason?" his secretary practically gushed. "So helpful. She told me where to find the diagram for the new addition to the library. You know, the one I've been looking for for two days. She told me it had slipped behind the copier and, sure enough, that's right where it was. Isn't that amazing?"

Jason gritted his teeth. "Just get me the sheriff, please."

Cherry Cooper, Lady Pandora to His Honor Mayor Jason Strong, grinned as she rode down in the elevator. Oh, the look on his face when she called him General. As the MasterCard commercial said: Priceless.

She bet not many people saw shock reflected in those intelligent blue eyes, on those chiseled features. With his bold cheekbones she suspected he had warrior blood in his history. Indian, Celt, Viking, she couldn't narrow it down, but she sensed he came from a long line of fighters.

He didn't shake easily; she'd give him his due there. Still, she'd rattled him a tad. More bluff than anything else. Body language and ego gave away a lot. Years of experience had taught her how to read a person almost as well as her psychic talent.

She already knew the good mayor was going to be a problem.

Not only because he refused to change his mind and let her into the fair, but because he made her palms itch.

Definitely not a good sign.

She'd known a month ago when she first visited Blossom that trouble would touch her here. Still, she hadn't counted on the distraction of a maverick in a suit.

How she wished she could hop on her bike and roll on down the road.

But her grandmother's health came first. The latest surgery had been successful, but her traveling days were over.

Wry humor tugged at Cherry's funny bone. It didn't take psychic powers to know the hunky mayor would not be happy to learn two fortune-tellers would soon be moving to his town.

Strolling out of City Hall into the Texas sunlight, Cherry slipped on her sunglasses and surveyed the picket-fence charm of Blossom's town square. She felt right at home with her black leather gear and bad girl Harley.

Yeah, right, as at home as a frog in a French chef's kitchen.

Who was she kidding? The good mayor was right; no matter how much she longed for a home, this wasn't the place for her.

No, her place was on the road, moving from town to town, fair to fair, bringing in the income.

But first she needed to secure her place in the Blossom County Fair. She and Nona had been pre-approved for a home loan, but one of the conditions was proof of six months of payment reserves in the bank at the time of closing. They'd saved over the years so they had enough for the down payment, but Nona's medical expenses had taken a chunk of their savings. In order to meet the loan condition, Cherry needed to get into the fair.

To do that, she needed the good people of Blossom on her side.

A woman jostled Cherry as she rushed down the City Hall steps. Cherry stared after the thin brunette, disturbed by the ominous shiver that followed in her wake.

Cherry's ability to see the future came mostly through touch. When she performed, she used tarot cards. Occasionally, if she felt the need to do a deeper reading, she'd use the guise of reading the client's palm, and then she buffered the contact with a scarf.

The contact with the rude woman reminded Cherry of the gray pall she'd felt when she first came to town. Shaking off the feeling of oppression, she cleansed her mind. Deciding to dive in at the deep end, she headed for The BeeHive Diner by way of the park.

She had an agenda to keep and it didn't include solving the town's dark problems. That was something for the good mayor to do.

The yellow-and-brown color scheme and honey-bee mural were charmingly cheerful. After placing her order, Cherry pulled out her cell phone and dialed her grandmother.

"Hey, Nona. You sound breathless, you're not doing anything you shouldn't are you?"

"What, and break a sweat? Where's the fun in that?" Nona responded.

A low male rumble sounded in the background.

"Oh, hush. I'm talking to my granddaughter," Nona's muffled voice admonished, then she spoke back into the phone. "I do everything my physical therapist tells me to do."

Again the rumble, which Nona ignored except for a giggle. A giggle!

"Enough about me. Did you reach Blossom? What did the mayor say?"

The mayor—dark hair, gray-blue eyes, wide shoulders, hard attitude.

"Not a sympathetic man, the mayor. Mostly he said he wouldn't change his mind, that the ban existed because the townspeople had been hurt by a fortune-teller in the past."

"That doesn't sound good."

"I did some research. Two years ago, a fortune-teller was on the take with a con man running a real estate scam. The fortune-teller planted the seed by telling people they would soon see a good investment, then a couple of weeks after the fair, a man breezed into town, the supposed representative of a development company ready to build a resort in the area. People lined up to buy. Next thing they knew, the fortune-teller was long gone, the resort didn't exist, and the man had disappeared along with half a million dollars of the good citizens' money."

"Charlatan." The lash of fury in Nona's voice traveled clearly down the line. She detested frauds. "And now we have to pay for her deceit."

"Unfortunately. But we can't really blame the people of Blossom for not wanting a repeat performance. Last year, they didn't have a fair at all."

"Well, now. That's just a shame. Those charlatans stole more than the town's money, they stole their spirit."

Nona truly believed in the positive energy to be had at the fair. Family values and young love, goodness and joy, all wrapped up in popcorn, cotton candy and hot summer nights were what made up the fair.

Cherry believed, too, but she also knew frauds existed, people spent what they couldn't afford and life wasn't always fair. Even at the fair.

"Don't worry," she reassured her grandmother. "I'm not giving up."

"What do you have planned?"

"A few innocent parlor tricks, is all. The people of Blossom may have been burnt, but curiosity will bring them back every time."

"There's something more, isn't there? Something in your voice—" Nona suddenly switched gears. "You've met someone haven't you? A man."

Cherry grimaced. She'd hoped to finish the conversation before it headed in this direction.

"Nona, didn't we have this talk when I was eighteen? I want to form my own opinion about the men I meet."

"We didn't have this talk. This isn't about the big bad wolf. We're talking Prince Charming here."

Oh, please. Cherry barely kept from saying the words out loud. Jason Strong might look like a prince, but charming he was not.

"Believe me, we are not talking Prince Charming. Take care of yourself, Nona. I'll call after I've been to the Realtor."

Nona hung up the phone, her thoughts still with her granddaughter until a voice broke into her musings.

"You were talking about men, right? With your granddaughter?" Tom Baxter asked. An ex-cop with broad shoulders and lots of pewter-colored hair, he was here recuperating from a blown-out knee. "I understand the reference to the Big Bad Wolf, but what does Prince Charming mean in this day and age?"

The big Texan's attention flustered Nona. Lord, she hadn't felt so nervous around a man since her Grant first courted her a million years ago. Sweet Grant, he'd been her Prince Charming. She'd known the first time he touched her he was her soul mate. They'd had twenty wonderful years together before she lost him to a heart attack. Now she was seventy-one and could barely walk across the room. She certainly had nothing to offer this Big Bad Wolf.

Still, she answered his question about Prince Charming. "It means her one true love."

Chapter Two

Leaving the BeeHive, Blossom pushed open the door and came face-to-face with Jason Strong.

"Lady Pandora." He held the door for her. "Still in town?"

"Mr. Mayor." She pasted a smile on her face; not all that hard to do when he was such an almighty joy to look at. She stepped past him onto the sidewalk. "Of course. I don't plan on going anywhere. I have a date with the fair in a few days."

His light blue eyes narrowed. "You shouldn't get your hopes up. I won't change my mind. Too many people stand to get hurt if I do."

Cherry just smiled more brightly; because he honestly didn't know the insult he'd dealt her. "I'm very careful not to hurt people. When you have a talent such as I have, you learn early that it comes with a responsibility to shield people from the answers they're so eager to hear."

"Very honorable of you. Except you're wasting your time. I don't believe in your special talents." He broke off to greet two ladies exiting the diner. "Mrs. White, Mrs. Davis, good afternoon."

The women were complete opposites one, tall, thin, and dark; the other, short, sturdy, and silver. They greeted their mayor, then turned twin looks of interest in Cherry's direction.

Unaffected, she met their stares. "Afternoon. Wasn't the apple cobbler exceptional?"

Brilliant smiles broke over their faces. The taller of the women rolled her eyes and patted her chest. "My, yes. The cobbler *was* delicious today."

"Excellent, just excellent," her companion voiced her opinion. "Just a tad too much cinnamon."

"Oh Mary Ellen, everything always has too much cinnamon for you."

"Well, I don't care for a lot of cinnamon." The two women moved on down the street, discussing the merits of spice versus flavoring.

Enjoying their good-natured squabbling, Cherry didn't notice the mayor's eyes had narrowed again until he stepped in front of her.

Her humor disappeared. "Oh, please. You think that was a demonstration? That was nothing, I saw them eating the cobbler. It looked good, so I ordered some. You want a demonstration, talk to your secre-

tary. Did she find the document she was looking for?
It had something to do with a city building." She
cocked her head, seeing by the look on his face that
his secretary had indeed found the missing papers.
"The library, I think."

Oh yeah, that nailed it. That had him thinking.
Emboldened, she invaded his space and lowered her
voice to a husky drawl.

"I can do even better than that."

Careful not to touch him—that would be too daring—she reached for his tie. Savoring the feel of silk
warm from the heat of his body, she slid the soft fab-
ric through her fingers. A low-volume buzz tingled
through her.

Hmm. That had never happened before.

Her eyes on his, she opened her senses the tiniest
bit. It didn't take much to connect with his energy;
to align with his nagging need to find a specific item.

One of the fastest ways to convert nonbelievers
was to help them find something. It was personal and
almost everyone had something they were looking
for at any given time. The nagging factor also helped.
Easier to pick up something that was close to the surface of someone's mind.

In Jason Strong's mind, she saw a ring. A wedding ring.

The mayor was married. Something inside her
flinched at the revelation. But no. He had been married. A widower, then. Because the sorrow she saw
in his eyes spoke of death.

Emotions bombarded her: loss, grief, sadness, anger, loneliness. Desire. Guilt. And an absolute resolve to keep her from the fair.

She dropped his tie and stepped back. Too much, too fast, too personal. And way too close for comfort. She'd seen way more than she usually allowed herself. Out of respect for him and self-defense for herself, she put even more distance between them.

"I'm sorry for your loss," she said softly.

His head went back in surprise and a frown slammed his eyebrows together. "What?"

She'd blocked his emotions, but hers were all over the place as well. Focusing on compassion, she shook her head and simply repeated, "I'm sorry." Then, because it would give him peace, she added. "You'll find what you're looking for under the nightstand beside your bed. The one on the right, by the back left leg."

Knowing she'd said more than enough, she turned and walked away.

"I want that woman gone." Jason slid into the gold-and-brown booth across from Sheriff Trace McCabe inside the BeeHive. Brown-haired, hazel-eyed, Trace had the look of the boy next door with a military edge. He had two traits Jason wanted in his sheriff—calm in a crisis and the perseverance of a bulldog. "What did you find?"

The younger man reached for his coffee, then nodded toward the door Jason had just come through. "That her?"

"Yeah." Feeling exposed after his run-in with the troublesome gypsy, Jason averted his gaze to the window overlooking City Hall Park. His gaze fell on the gazebo and he made a mental note to check with Parks and Recreations on the search for the fair banner. With the fair due to start in about a week, the banner should have been up a month ago.

"She seemed awfully friendly."

Focusing on his friend, Jason nodded at the file on the table. "What did you find out about Lady Pandora?"

Trace cocked his head but allowed the evasion. "Well, for starters, her real name is Blossom Ann Cooper. Goes by Cherry. Bet she took some ribbing for that. Here's the interesting part. She was born twenty-six years ago right here in Blossom City. Her mother died from complications of childbirth. Other than that only a few nuisance offenses in her youth, they didn't even bother to seal the record. Nothing beyond a speeding ticket in the last ten years."

Stunned by the revelation she'd been born in Blossom, Jason said, "I saw her arrive on a Harley this morning."

Trace shrugged. "Nothing against the law in that."

"I know. I just… She was born in Blossom? That's a bit of a coincidence, don't you think?" Jason didn't like the sound of this, not one bit.

"Too much of one for my comfort, but I couldn't find anything to indicate she's up to anything. Her address is a P.O. box in Florida. Besides the Harley, she has a fifth-wheel trailer and a Ford truck in her name and that of Rose Cooper, her grandmother. Cherry was given into Rose's custody after her mother died. They work the fair routes together."

"Where's her grandmother now?"

Trace set down his coffee. "No file on her yet. Nothing of interest, anyway. They usually travel together, so she's probably at the last fair they worked. I'm pulling the security checks we did. This troupe has the best reputation in the country, but we'll go back, ask specifically about the fortune-tellers."

Jason nodded. "In the meantime, keep an eye on her, will you? Let me know if she leaves town."

"You'll be the first to know." Trace cocked his index finger at Jason, a sign they'd developed ages ago indicating Jason owed Trace a beer for his efforts.

"Sheriff, Mayor, just the gentlemen I've been looking for." Bitsy Dupres stopped next to their table. The pale, blond woman wore a dark gray pantsuit, appearing colorless in the cheerful honeybee-themed diner.

Bitsy still mourned her late husband. To fill her days, she'd taken on the self-appointed task of keeping Blossom's children safe. With a few other overzealous citizens, she'd formed the Committee for Moral Behavior. A worthy cause for certain, except if left up to them, the children of Blossom would be wrapped up in cotton wool and tucked away in their rooms for safe keeping.

"Good afternoon, Bitsy," Trace returned her greeting. "What can we do for you?"

"I wondered if you had any news for me regarding the CMB's request to have the carnival banned from the fair this year."

"Bitsy." Jason reached down deep for patience. "We've explained that it's too late to ban the carnival."

"Yes. But I believe the morals of our children are more important than the few dollars involved in breaking a contract."

"More than a few dollars. The economy can't absorb another hit."

"So it's of no matter that the children will be exposed to a bad element? Everyone knows these carnival people are little better than transients and thieves. Look at what happened with poor Melissa Tolliver."

Trace fielded that one. "It's not like you, Bitsy, to be so judgmental. Let me reassure you this troupe is the best in the country. They may travel from town to town, but they are professionals at what they do."

"I'm afraid that's not good enough." Bitsy's shoulders went back and pink tinged her cheeks from the sheriff's gentle rebuke. "Trouble is what they are. I can assure you, you'll be hearing more about this from the committee."

Tucking her gray purse into the crook of her elbow, she inclined her head. "Good day, gentleman."

Full dark had fallen by the time Jason carried his daughter, Rikki, into the house that night. He dropped his briefcase inside the door, adjusted her slight weight against his shoulder, and carried her upstairs.

She didn't stir once, not even when he laid her on the bed. She lay with arms sprawled, half turned on her side. If he left her like this, she'd still be in the same position when he came in to wake her tomorrow morning.

The girl had two speeds, full tilt and full stop.

He envied the first and lived for the second. Just looking at her made his heart melt, but sometimes he loved her best just like this, blessedly still and blessedly quiet.

Hard to believe she'd be three in a week.

He pulled off her shoes and socks, amazed at the dirt accumulated in both. He replaced her shirt and shorts with bunny pajamas, giving her a quick swipe with a disposable wet cloth in between—what his mother didn't know couldn't hurt him—then he tucked her between the sheets.

He bent to kiss her soft curls. When he rose and turned, he caught sight of the picture on the dresser.

His wife, Diane. Taken when they were on a ski trip in Colorado.

He lifted the frame, angled it so the light from the hall caught it. Her cheeks were rosy, her eyes bright with laughter, her blond hair tucked under a red-and-white knit cap. They'd still lived in Lubbock when the picture was taken, before she'd gotten pregnant.

They'd lived for the moment then, lived for each other. Those had been the best of times.

She'd been so happy to learn she was expecting Rikki. It's what they both wanted. A family. A lifetime together. They'd moved back to Blossom City as their life plan dictated. They opened an office, he practiced law and Diane and his sister Hannah sold real estate.

Then Rikki was born. Their beautiful baby girl. A miracle. Life was good, the best ever.

Then it was over. Gone. The heart of his life destroyed by an accident. Rikki's mother stolen from them because she was in the wrong place at the wrong time. A car crossed the median when the driver suffered a heart attack.

And suddenly Jason was alone with a one-month-old baby girl. He hadn't had time to grieve, to mourn the loss of his wife. His life.

He'd missed Diane so much.

Still did. Or the long, lean lady in leather wouldn't get to him so easily.

He'd handled Diane's loss just like he'd handled every crisis in his life—by taking one day at a time, following a routine, keeping everyone close and accounted for.

So why did he have the feeling life was slipping out of his control? Maybe because his mother had run off to Europe with Aunt Stella. Or because his sister had become secretive lately. Or just because his baby was growing up.

It couldn't be because he'd begun to chafe under his own need for control. Keeping life on track meant keeping his loved ones safe.

He set the picture down, pulled the door half-closed and made his way down the hall to his room.

He dated, more out of expedience than for romance. But the women knew the score, and he had no desire for entanglements. Especially not a sultry brunette with a talent for riling his temper. And for sticking her nose where it didn't belong.

Just to prove her wrong, he went to the nightstand to the right of his bed, and lifted it away from the wall. Fully prepared to find nothing.

Almost hoping to find nothing.

No such luck. Gold sparkled against the dark blue carpeting.

Bending, he scooped up his wedding ring, flung in guilty rage the first night he went out with another woman and had more than dinner with her. He'd gotten over the guilt of living when Diane died. Yet losing the symbol of their love had stuck with him.

Finding the ring helped.

Being attracted to the sexy gypsy that helped him find it was another thing altogether.

Two days later, after making arrangements for Carlo Fuentes to drive her rig into Blossom when the troupe came to town in a few days, Cherry walked into the Cut N Curl.

No better place to jump into the thick of things in a small town than the local beauty parlor.

The bell over the door jingled. Orange, yellow and pink bright enough to require sunglasses greeted her along with a cheerful hello from a tiny woman with a big voice and big hair the same color as the orange seats.

"Welcome to the Cut N Curl. I'm Wanda Mae." A blast of hairspray accompanied her words.

"Do you take walk-ins?" Cherry asked. As she'd hoped, the place was packed with women in the process of beautifying themselves.

"Well, of course we do. Hang on just a sec."

Cherry took a seat and absorbed the scene. Besides Wanda Mae, two other women worked on hair while another three did nails. A posted sign advertised everything from waxing to tattooing.

Tattooing? My, my, weren't they progressive in Blossom?

Wanda Mae whipped the protective cover from the lap of her customer, an older woman with decidedly pink hair piled into a helmet of curls. "All done, Miss Ellie. You're all set to turn Big Al's eye at bingo tonight."

The woman had to be close to eighty, yet she twittered like a teenager. "Do you have any of that peppermint pink lipstick? Peppermint pink drives Big Al wild."

"'Course we do." Wanda Mae rang up the order, then sent Miss Ellie on her way with a few wise words. "You practice safe sex, you hear?"

Progressive indeed.

Cherry bit back a grin and put in her request for a pedicure. Wanda Mae warned Cherry there was a wait, then directed her to a massage chair with a basin at the foot.

She didn't mind waiting. It gave her a chance to observe and get acquainted. Smiling easily, she introduced herself as Lady Pandora to the woman next to her. Minnie Dressler, plump and past sixty, wore her gray hair held back by barrettes. They chatted, Cherry making sure to mention how sad she was not to be performing at the fair.

Then she sat back and opened a magazine. Sneaking a glance over the top every once in a while.

She saw suspicion, she'd expected that, but she also saw curiosity and interest in the glances sent her way.

Twenty minutes later, the whispers about her had faded away. The door opened, the bell jingled and a very pregnant blonde with a cranky toddler in tow entered the shop.

The women went into full cluck mode.

The expectant mama, Tammy, received a rush of attention. The crying baby plucked from her arms, she was helped into a seat, her feet lifted.

The toddler calmed down under the immediate barrage of attentiveness, but after being passed from woman to woman his mood began to suffer.

Cherry's heart went out to little Jimmy. Within the troupe, she was known to have a talent for healing, for having a special touch with babies.

Some day she hoped to have a career as a midwife. She hadn't spoken of that particular dream in a while. It upset Nona to think Cherry hesitated because of her. In truth Nona was only part of the problem. Cowardice accounted for the other part.

Cherry preferred not to dwell on either.

She longed to cuddle Jimmy, to ease his distress, but felt that would be pressing her luck.

He had other ideas. He looked at Cherry from the lap of her neighbor, his brown eyes dewy with tears. She smiled at him, and he slid down to stand in front of Cherry.

"Hello, Jimmy." He had fine blond hair and couldn't be more than eighteen months old. She leaned forward. "My name is Cherry."

He tugged a lock of her hair. "Pretty."

"Thank you." She carefully removed her hair from his chubby little fist.

"Up." Jimmy held his arms up.

Cherry's heart melted. She met his mother's gaze. "May I?" she asked. "I'm good with kids, and I'd like to help."

Tammy studied her for a moment, then nodded.

Smiling gently, Cherry lifted the boy into her lap. He immediately went exploring. He pulled her earrings, fiddled with her watch and the crystals in her bracelet. She did enjoy her baubles.

Eventually, he laid his head on her shoulder and fell asleep.

"Poor little tyke, he's tuckered out." Wanda Mae started the water in the whirlpool. "Do you want the massage? I recommend level three." She winked. "We call it the Erogenous Zone."

Mmm. Sounded tempting. Her erogenous zones could certainly use some attention. Now why did that bring to mind the dark hair and blue-gray eyes of Jason Strong?

"I'd better not. It might disturb Jimmy."

"Oh, Miss Pandora." Tammy pushed to her feet. "You need to do the massage. I'll take Jimmy." She arched her back.

She stood close and Cherry felt her tension, her exhaustion, her pain. More, Cherry felt the baby's readiness to be born. Tomorrow morning, Tammy would be holding her little girl in her arms.

Tammy reached for Jimmy. "I'm just glad he got a bit of a nap."

Cherry waved her away. "He's fine. Let him sleep. Have a manicure. It'll be a while before you get another chance."

Both Tammy and Wanda Mae gave Cherry odd looks.

She simply smiled serenely. "Trust me, when it comes to predicting births, I'm never wrong."

Not at this anyway. She always knew when an expectant mother would deliver. Even as she appreciated the gift, she recognized the cosmic joke. She'd lost her mother because she'd gone into labor in the middle of nowhere. Cherry had not come easily into the world. By the time they got her mother to Blossom, it was too late to save her.

Yet her daughter had the talent to make sure the same thing never happened to anyone she knew.

To Tammy, Cherry said, "You'd better pack your suitcase when you get home because you're going into the hospital tonight."

The announcement shook the rafters. Everyone started talking at once. "Cherry, you need to ante up for the baby pool," someone suggested.

"What's the pool up to?" Cherry didn't believe in using her talents to gamble, but if she won, the word of mouth would really help her cause.

"Two hundred twenty-two dollars. It's two dollars a guess. Tammy knows it's another boy, so you just need to guess the date, time, weight and height."

Another boy? Cherry ruminated on that for a moment, but no, it didn't feel right.

Thirty minutes later, Cherry logged in her official guess: tomorrow at 6:58 in the morning, Tammy would give birth to a seven-pound, two-ounce, nineteen-inch baby girl.

Word spread all over town. The fortune-teller instigated an uprising over at the Cut N Curl. Seems she'd thumbed her nose at modern medicine by predicting Tammy Wright would have a girl when the doctor said she'd be having a boy.

Cherry had said she'd take her case to the people; now Jason knew what she meant. She sure had a talent for making a big splash. And for making his life miserable.

He needed to put a stop to this now.

He found her at the Dairy Dream, an ice cream

and burger joint with a blue-and-silver, moon-and-stars theme. Rikki particularly liked the glow in the dark stars on the navy ceiling.

Cherry sat tucked up in a booth in the corner. She read a book, a romance by the look of the cover. She wore blue jeans and a white, off-the-shoulder peasant shirt. Her waves of dark curls were subdued into a loose braid.

Little fool, didn't she understand she risked the people turning on her? Courtesy of the Swindle, he'd dealt with angry crowds more than once. The thought of Cherry facing down a mob turned his blood cold. She might act tough, but he could span her waist with his hands and her long, slim neck, enticingly revealed by the wide-necked shirt, had a decidedly delicate look to it.

He slid in across from her, stretching his long legs in front of him. She glanced from the page to him. Immediately, pleasure lit up her eyes and she flashed him a smile.

Whoa Nellie. He took the impact right in the gut. God she was beautiful.

In the next instant, she returned her attention to her book, carefully marking her place and setting it on the banquette next to her. She shifted in her seat, pulling her legs up to sit Indian fashion. When she looked up again, the intensity of her welcome had dimmed. Those lovely dark chocolate eyes were once more guarded and her smile held a rueful edge.

"Good evening, Mayor." She pushed her fries toward him. "You look like you need something to gnaw on. Have a fry."

"I'm not here to chew you out." He reached for a golden fry dusted with crystals of salt. He grunted. Nobody did burgers and fries better than the Dairy Dream. "Hey, Stan," he hollered over the noise of the patrons, "bring me a burger to go with these fries."

Stan, the owner, waved an acknowledgement. Jason pulled his wallet out and set a five on the table. He helped himself to another fry.

"Well, you've been busy."

She shrugged and the sleeve slipped lower on her shoulder exposing creamy skin. He tried not to look, not to be tempted. Not to want her.

He had his daughter, his mom and his sister to care for and keep him company, and the town to keep him busy. That's all he needed, all he could handle.

His boring life suited him fine. In fact, he'd worked hard to achieve boring. Losing his wife had been brutal, facing each new morning alone was difficult, raising his daughter alone was hard. So yeah, he savored his peace.

Giving in to his attraction for this woman threatened the balance he'd fought so hard to achieve.

He dragged his gaze back to Cherry's face and his mind back to the matter at hand.

"You're causing an uproar in my town, Ms. Cooper."

"Since we're getting to be so cozy—" she reached for a fry, dipped it in ketchup, then bit it in half "—call me Cherry."

"Cherry. That's an unusual name. Especially since I know your real name is Blossom."

She cleared her throat. "My mom named me after the city I was born in so I could always find my way back to her. She died giving birth to me here in Blossom City. I had red hair when I was born. My grandmother called me Cherry Blossom. The Cherry stuck."

"Okay, Cherry." The pleasure the small intimacy gave him was probably not a good thing. "You're causing an uproar in my town."

She smiled and pointed a fry at him. "You have the power to change that."

"You're playing with fire. These people have been hurt. There's no telling how they're going to react to your shenanigans."

"What's wrong, Mayor—"

"Jason." He interrupted. "Call me Jason."

"Jason." She inclined her head in acknowledgement. "What's wrong? Are you afraid I'm going to prove myself?"

"I'm afraid you're going to get hurt." The truth in his statement surprised him. When exactly had he moved over to her side? No, that wasn't right. He wasn't taking sides. He was keeping the peace.

"What happens when you don't win the baby pool? You're going to be seen as a fool. Worse, people are going to be reminded of the Swindle and they're going to take their anger out on you."

"That's not a problem. I'm going to win the baby pool."

He thought of his wedding ring, found under the nightstand on the right of his bed just as she'd said. Maybe she could win the pool. "Winning may be worse for you than losing. Then it'll be another fortune-teller taking their money again. You can't win."

A teenager with an unfortunate case of acne brought over Jason's burger. The boy scooped up Jason's five.

"Keep the change, Johnny."

The boy grinned and snapped the five taut. "Thanks, Mayor."

Cherry waited until the boy left them alone before claiming, "I know what I'm doing."

"Are you sure? Have you ever dealt with a mob? It's not pretty."

Totally calm, she responded, "That won't happen."

"You don't know that." He bit into his burger.

She simply gazed at him from those fabulous, knowing eyes. He gritted his teeth in frustration. He didn't have to be psychic to know he wasn't getting through to her.

"Where's your grandmother? She usually travels with you doesn't she?"

Surprise followed by wariness flashed across her fine-boned features. "She does, yes."

He waited, but she didn't elaborate. "Will she be joining you soon?"

"No."

Again, nothing followed. "You know for a woman who makes her living talking with people, you aren't very forthcoming."

She leaned forward, her forearms bracketing the cooling plate of fries, her eyes intent. "Do you want your fortune told, Jason?"

Did she think to intimidate him? He leaned toward her, his arms framing hers. "Is that the only way you allow someone to get close? By reading them?"

She held her position, though he saw it cost her. "I don't get close to those I read. It gets in the way of my sight."

"So who do you get close to?" Now why did he ask that? Hadn't he just lectured himself on the need for objectivity around this stunning gypsy? "You don't have to answer that."

She shrugged one nearly bare shoulder, then casually retreated back into her seat. "My friends are the carnies we travel with."

It couldn't be more clear where her loyalties lay. "So it's all an act when you're making nice and getting buddy-buddy with the townspeople? Just a means to the end? It all comes down to the money, doesn't it? And you wonder why I don't want you in the fair?"

"I don't wonder at all." She grabbed her book and purse and scooted to the edge of the bench seat. "It's obvious you've made up your mind about me. Well, I won't apologize for my profession. Yes, I take money, for a service. And people get their money's worth." She rose to stand next to the table.

"I'm not going to go away, Jason. And if you refuse to let me in the fair, you'd better be prepared for the consequences."

She turned on her heel, but he reached out and caught her sleeve stopping her. "What's that mean?"

"It means there's a shop for rent on Main Street." Pulling free, she wove her way to the door and disappeared into the darkness outside.

Oh Lord, he was in trouble. Not because she'd threatened to open up a business in his town, but because, God, he did admire gutsy women.

Chapter Three

Cherry discreetly checked her watch. Still plenty of time. She had an appointment with the realtor in thirty minutes. She'd left her motel early to stop by the BeeHive for breakfast, then walk through the park.

She'd won the baby pool yesterday, and what good was there in stirring up the waters if you weren't out swirling them in the direction you wanted them to go?

"Ladies, thank you so much for your support. Make sure to tell Mayor Strong how you feel, and I'll save you an appointment at the fair." She waved her goodbyes to Mrs. White and Mrs. Davis and strolled for the corner that gave access to Cypress Street.

The pretty day added to her joy in the morning. Blue skies, the scent of fresh-cut grass on the air, and a breeze playful enough to lift the hem of her navy-and-turquoise paisley skirt made her think of home.

An odd reaction, when the only home she'd ever known had four wheels and an awning. Maybe she was enjoying these days in Blossom City a little too much. The place, the people, they were getting to her when she knew better than to let herself care.

"Missy. Yeah, Missy, over here." An age-roughened voice hailed Cherry from a few feet away.

She followed the sound and found two elderly men in overalls and plaid shirts seated on a bench at the edge of the park. Both men had gray hair, though one had more than the other. But then he had more of a paunch, too. Each claimed an end of the bench with a two-foot space separating them. On the sidewalk exactly half way between them sat a tobacco-stained coffee can.

As she neared them, she saw the biggest similarity was the twin sparks of deviltry deep in their eyes. These two had seen a bit of trouble in their day. And caused a little, too.

"You're the carnival gal, yeah?" The taller of the two waved her closer. "The fortune-teller? We want our fortunes told. I'm Dutch, that there's Buster."

Hands on her hips, she assessed the two characters. If she gave them half a chance, they'd have her running in circles. "Sure. I predict, a new coffee can in your future."

"Huh. No news there." Buster revealed his skepticism. "Bea over to the BeeHive gives us a new can once a week."

"Now hold on. No way she knew that. Seems to me we got the real deal here." Dutch rubbed his hands together. "Go on, do your thing."

Cherry hid her amusement. "Gentlemen, exactly what do you want to know?"

Both men looked to the left, then to the right.

"There's a conspiracy to get us moved off our bench. Damn Moral Misfits," Dutch whispered loudly. "We've been sitting on this here bench longer than some of them been around. They got no call to be buttin' their noses in where we sit."

"No call." Buster agreed.

"What we want, Madam Peacock, is for you to look into your crystal ball and tell us how to get the damn Crappy Committee off our backs."

"Well now. I don't have my crystal ball with me, but let's see what I can do." Ceremoniously, Cherry circled the bench three times.

"Yeah now, gal, you're making me dizzy. You got something to tell us or what?"

Nothing special happened by circling except to give her a chance to think, to feel. Unfortunately, the two men had built up too many shields through the years for her to read them. Which meant falling back on body language, and good sense.

Seriously, what harm were these two fixtures?

"Dutch, Buster." She paused for dramatic effect. "From what I see, you're a match for all comers."

"Hee hee," Dutch slapped his knee. "I told you she was the real deal."

"Huh, you bet your sweet patooty we are." Buster cackled his delight. A truly disquieting sound. Cherry suddenly pitied the committee.

Smiling to herself, she wished them a good day and moved on. She hadn't gone far when she felt the weight of his eyes on her.

She always knew when Jason watched her. His gaze flowed over her light as a touch, intense as a kiss. He caused her skin to tingle and her mouth to water, making her wonder what he tasted like.

Then she wised up and remembered he represented everything she wasn't: conservative, established, grounded.

He was also determined, protective and ruled by duty. All admirable qualities, except when they kept her out of the fair.

She stopped and did a slow spin, looking, looking.

Ah, there he was. The good mayor stood on the steps of City Hall talking to a park worker. But oh yeah, his eyes were on her.

Holding his gaze, she changed directions, boldly stalking him.

"Do the best you can," Jason told the worker, never taking his attention off her. "And find the fair banner. I want it found and hung by the end of the day."

"Jeez, Jason, I don't know about that." The worker lifted his ball cap, swept a hand over his head, replaced the hat. "We've looked everywhere."

"Look again."

"Problems finding something, Mayor?" Cherry

asked, all innocent helpfulness. "I'm really good at finding things."

"No, thank you." He stated, but a voice piped up from behind him.

"That's a wonderful idea, Jason." Minnie Dressler joined them. The red barrettes holding back her gray hair matched the trim on her black-and-white checked dress. She patted Jason's arm. "You should have thought of this sooner."

She turned a smile of eager anticipation on Cherry. "Lady Pandora, remember me? We met at the Cut N Curl. I was over at the BeeHive earlier when you helped Clyde find his sunglasses. I'm on the fair board, responsible for the publicity. I'd be ever so thankful if you could help us find that banner."

"Minnie," Jason protested. "We'll find the banner. We don't need help."

Minnie propped her hands on ample hips and faced off with His Honor. "We've been looking for over a month. If we haven't found it by now, we're not going to." She turned her energy on Cherry. "You go on, honey, and do your thing."

Minnie crossed her arms over her chest and waited.

Aware of Jason's attention, Cherry drew on her sense of professionalism. She smiled at each of the three people focused on her. "I usually work with the person who actually lost the item, but we'll see what we can do. I'll need your help."

She climbed up one step, then asked Minnie to

stand in front of her. Cherry placed the worker on her right. A reluctant Jason stood to her left. "Now I need each of you to picture the banner, while I concentrate."

Cherry closed her eyes and immediately smelled Jason's scent, a masculine musk that tickled her senses and made her blood warm. No doubt about it, the man was yummy.

Pushing aside her physical reaction, she opened her mind reaching for a vision of the banner. From either side of her, she felt the energy growing, connecting them.

The mayor came across clear as a blank wall. Helpful as ever.

Breathe in through the nose, out through the mouth. Again. A picture appeared of the banner hanging over the gazebo. She concentrated, yet her mind's eye stayed on the gazebo. Which, she'd learned, often provided an answer in itself. She followed that path and found what she sought.

She opened her eyes.

Minnie stood directly in front of Cherry, her eyes closed, hands upraised, palms up as if making an offering to the fates. The worker on the right stood with head bowed and eyes closed. No special sight needed to read his wish to be anywhere but here.

Jason stood eyes open, feet braced apart, arms crossed over his chest, challenge stamped on his features, in full combat mode.

Cherry winked at him.

He scowled. "Are you done?"

Minnie's eyes popped open. She clasped her hands together and leaned closer to Cherry. "Well?"

Cherry eyed the mayor speculatively. "If I get this right, do I get my place in the fair?"

"Yes." Minnie piped in.

"No." Jason turned his scowl on his fellow fair board member. "First, she hasn't done anything yet. Second, you don't have the authority to okay that."

Minnie scowled right back at him. "I have the authority to bring it up at tonight's meeting. With the fair board's approval, only you stand in her way. We need that banner, Jason."

"I don't respond to blackmail." No backing down there. "What about your friend Bitsy?" he asked Minnie. "The Committee for Moral Behavior won't be happy to see a fortune-teller in the fair."

The Committee for Moral Behavior? That didn't sound good. Minnie didn't think so, either, by the look on her face.

The worker actually paled.

Was this the same committee trying to displace Dutch and Buster? Cherry disliked the sound of it more and more.

Determination replaced Minnie's momentary doubts. "Bitsy doesn't want anyone at the fair. She means well, but sometimes she overreacts."

Cherry decided she better end this before she lost further ground.

"There's no need to get dramatic." She waved a nonchalant hand. "In the spirit of cooperation, I'm willing to share the information. The banner is in the gazebo."

"*In* the gazebo?" Minnie voiced her confusion.

"There's a storage space under the base," the worker spoke up. He lifted his hat, swept back his hair. "I've already looked there."

Cherry softened her insistence with a smile. "You need to look deeper. On the left side. Right against the gazebo wall."

He just stared at her for a moment, then turned to Jason for direction.

Jason looked pained, but shrugged. "Go ahead, check it out."

"Now." Minnie demanded. "Let's check it now." Not waiting for anyone, she started down the steps. "Bring the keys," she called over her shoulder, and the worker went trotting after her.

Jason met Cherry's gaze. "I don't understand how you can keep setting yourself up for public failure."

"You keep lacking faith in me."

"You can't be right all the time."

"Of course not," she responded honestly. "I know my limitations. Which means when I choose to go public, you shouldn't doubt me."

His eyes narrowed, disbelief and exasperation in the gray depths. Poor man, he really was out of his element when it came to the psychic world. Good. She needed every advantage she could exploit to fight him.

Feeling smug she'd bested him this time, she put

a little extra swing into her hips on her way down the steps. She looked at him over her shoulder.

"We'll just call this one a freebie."

Cherry practically skipped down the sidewalk toward the yellow house, third from the corner on Cypress Street. She hoped the Realtor had waited. They were scheduled to look at three houses this morning.

Nona had three demands when it came to her new home—a yard, a big kitchen and two baths. She'd spent the last fifty years of her life sharing a small trailer and a smaller bathroom. She didn't intend to ever share again.

Cherry could relate.

The yard caught her attention first. A lush carpet of green ran from the flowerbed fronting the house to the street. A red brick walk wound through the grass to the matching brick wall. Charming. Her grandmother hadn't mentioned roses, but Cherry imagined she'd cope.

She pushed open the red picket gate and headed down the brick walk toward the door. It opened before she reached it and a blue-eyed, brown-haired pixie popped out.

"Hi," she said, her head cocked back so her curls trailed down her back. "Are you the fruit?"

"Hello," Cherry responded. "What's your name?"

"Rikki." She spun around in a circle making her pink tutu flare. "My birthday is this many days." She held up seven fingers. Then spun again. "I'll be three."

Cherry grinned. Rikki was too adorable. "Do you live here, Rikki?"

"Uh-uh." When she faced front, she bowed. "Are you the fruit?"

Fruit? Ah. "My name is Cherry."

She smiled and clapped. "You're here. You're here." She turned and ran inside. "She's here. She's here."

Cherry stepped inside behind the little girl. "Hello?"

"In here," a feminine voice came from the back of the house.

Taking time to assess the rooms as she went, Cherry walked through the living room and an archway into a dining room, both rooms were flooded with light from large windows. French doors stood open onto the kitchen.

The kitchen was not large, but had a window seat with a card table pushed up to it—the only furniture in the house—and Cherry could see the possibility for a breakfast nook. Yellow was in here, too, a soft, creamy yellow that absorbed the sunlight and made the room bright and welcoming. The appliances, counters and cupboards were white, as was the trellis wound with green ivy stenciled on the wall on either side of the window seat.

Okay, so the room wasn't exactly large, but the window seat really opened it up. Plus, when you were used to a kitchen the size of a postage stamp, large was relative.

Rikki danced around a tall, slim woman with

lovely caramel-brown hair who sat at the card table. Papers covered the surface in front of her. She looked up, and Cherry saw where the little girl got her blue eyes.

"Ms. Cooper, I'm Hannah Brown." She stood and offered her hand. She wore a deep pink jacket over a white T-shirt and jeans, appearing comfortable yet chic. Cherry took Hannah's hand.

"I'm Cherry." As soon as skin touched skin, Cherry sensed the underlying joy, hope and fear the woman hid behind her surface calm. "I'm sorry to be late."

As quickly and as casually as possible, Cherry broke the contact. But not before she sensed the growing child and the anxiety of a mother fearing the loss of another baby.

Rarely did she allow the intimacy of skin-to-skin contact, to prevent just such an intrusion as with Hannah.

"Ms. Cooper? Cherry?" Hannah called her name, obviously not for the first time.

"This place is wonderful." Cherry smiled and glanced around as if her distraction had been the house and not a glimpse into the woman's private life.

Damn, she hated when this happened. Now she didn't know whether to ignore what she'd seen, or say something even though she hadn't been asked for advice.

Hannah held her arms wide. "It has everything you asked for, a yard both front and back, a nice-sized kitchen, and two-and-a-half baths. Just two bedrooms, though. But they are both master suites with attached baths and walk-in closets."

"A walk-in closet?" The decadent thought actually distracted Cherry from her dilemma. Heck, it was almost enough to make her think of giving up the road.

"This way, this way." Rikki ran down a hall that led to the back of the house.

Cherry met Hannah's gaze as they turned to follow the pink bundle of energy. "She's adorable," Cherry tried to see behind Hannah's calm facade. "She's very precocious."

"She is." Hannah laughed. "Both adorable and precocious, but I only have her on loan. She's my niece. I'm watching her for my brother." Her smile dimmed, took a brave turn. "My husband and I haven't been blessed with a child yet."

That did it. Cherry couldn't resist the wistfulness in the woman's voice. Not when she could give her peace of mind. But she'd wait until they'd completed their business today. And then she'd give Hannah the choice.

Two hours later, they were back at the yellow house. Cherry had made up her mind. She wanted this house, but she'd wait to commit. She knew better than to appear too eager. This was a big decision, and not hers alone to make. She'd take tonight, then call Nona tomorrow.

But it was all a formality. This would be Nona's new home.

She faced Hannah. "Thank you for your help today. You've been a great help."

"Hey, that's why you'll be paying me the big bucks. I can see you love this place. Come inside and we'll write up the offer." Hannah handed Cherry the keys. "You get the door, I'll get Sleeping Beauty."

Halfway through the tour of the third house Rikki had climbed into Cherry's arms and fallen asleep. Now she slept on the window seat while Cherry told Hannah she'd like to think about it.

A professional, Hannah took the news in stride. "Just let me know when you're ready to go looking again."

"I will." Rather than reach for her purse, Cherry reached for Hannah's hand. Meeting her blue eyes, Cherry allowed her compassion to show.

"You've helped me, now I wish to help you. I've a talent for seeing the direction of the future. It's not a certain future, but the likely future if your life remains on its current course." She squeezed the fingers within her hold. "Will you allow me to give you a reading?"

Hannah stared at Cherry, assessing her sincerity. "You're Lady Pandora aren't you? You won the baby pool yesterday morning. I heard you gave the winnings to Tammy. That was very generous of you."

Cherry shrugged modestly. "I have a talent. For instance, I know you're expecting a child."

Hannah blinked and fell back a step. "Yes. But I haven't told anyone yet."

"You're afraid you may lose the child."

Her cheeks paled. "Yes. I've miscarried twice. I

can't bear losing another baby." Her hand shielding her abdomen, she lifted pleading eyes to Cherry. "Tell me truthfully, will I ever hold my baby in my arms?"

"Remember," Cherry cautioned, "what I see is a probable future, but if you follow the directions of your doctor, I see that you will, yes."

"What the hell is going on here?" A deep male voice demanded, fury ground into each word.

Cherry flinched but kept her voice casual as she asked Hannah, "Do you happen to know Mayor Jason Strong?"

Hannah nodded. "He's my brother."

"Ah." Darn. Cherry cursed the talent that helped others yet failed to warn her when she'd stepped into the mire. "Please tell me his bark is worse than his bite."

Hannah bit her lip and worry wrinkled her brow. "Not when it comes to family."

"Great." Cherry turned to face the man bearing down on her, the move adroitly placing Hannah between Cherry and Jason. No way she'd let him touch her with that much anger near the surface. "Good afternoon, Jason."

"I want to talk to you." He circled his sister, tracking Cherry.

"I was just leaving." She matched him step for step, keeping Hannah between them.

"You're not going anywhere." Eyes cold as ice and just as sharp sliced through Cherry, but he was all gentleness when he spoke to his sister. "Hannah, pay no attention to what she told you. Take Rikki to my car for me. I'll be there in a moment. After Lady Pandora and I have a word."

Hannah sidestepped into his path. "Jason, she's done nothing wrong."

"She's playing you, Hannah, pretending an interest in property to get to you, and through you to me. Well, she's overplayed her hand."

"That's not true." Hannah denied his allegation. "She's buying this house. I won't allow you to harangue her. Not when she's been nothing but nice to me."

Rather than appease him, her news had the opposite effect. His eyes narrowed to suspicious slits. Putting a hand on each of her upper arms, he moved his sister out of his way.

"Please take Rikki out to the car," he repeated.

"It's all right, Hannah. He's just trying to protect you. I'll talk to him." Lifting her chin in defiance, she challenged him. "There's no need to worry. I'm sure he'll be a true gentleman."

Hannah still hesitated. "Jason?"

Gritting his teeth, he nodded. "I'll be charm itself."

"See that you are." Hannah retrieved her niece and her briefcase. "Lock up when you're done."

Watching her buffer walk out the door, Cherry drew on every bit of her strength not to take a huge step backward, especially when he narrowed the distance between them.

Standing so close his anger breathed down on her, he demanded, "What the hell are you up to?"

"Nothing nefarious as you seem to think. I felt your sister's anxiety. I just wanted to reassure her."

"Stay away from Hannah. She's in a fragile condition, and I won't allow you to give her false hope. If you're looking to impress me, you've chosen the wrong way."

His knowledge threw her. "How do you know she's pregnant? She said she hadn't told anyone."

His head snapped back in surprise. "She's pregnant?" He cursed creatively. "You better not have said anything to hurt her."

Darn it. Darn him. Now he'd made her break Hannah's confidence. Okay, so he cared about his sister and didn't want to see her hurt. Fine. Great. Cherry respected that, but this attack was both unfounded and unwarranted. He didn't know what he was talking about, and he'd put her on the defensive causing her to reveal something that wasn't hers to tell. Well, no more.

She made a point of honoring people's privacy. If they elected to tell what they learned during a reading, that was their choice. Annoyed with him for making her break her own rule, she quit retreating and took the offensive.

"Back up, mister."

She poked him in the middle of his burgundy-and-gray striped tie, noting in the back of her mind the increased wattage generated by the contact, due no doubt to the level of his rage added to the usual awareness crackling in the air around them.

"You tricked me. You made it sound like you knew she was pregnant. You better act surprised when she tells you. And you will not attack her like you are me regarding our conversation. That's private and doesn't concern you."

He leaned into her poking finger. "Don't dictate to me. This is my sister we're talking about."

"That doesn't make it your business. Yes, she is fragile regarding the subject of this baby, but she's a strong woman and she can handle whatever she needs to handle. That doesn't mean you need to put that to the test by putting her on the defensive." She poked him again for good measure.

"I object to you speaking to her at all. And what did she mean when she said you bought this house?"

"None of your business."

Wrong thing to say. He pushed right past her pointed finger to put his face inches from hers, digging into her with those laser-sharp eyes. Even the tips of his ears turned red. "The hell it's not. It's my sister and my town. Now talk. Are you going to buy this house?"

"I might." Her chin went up again, daring him to make something of it. "I'm thinking about it."

"You better think long and hard, lady. Because if you're not serious about any offer you put on this place, I'll see you arrested for fraud."

"You'd like that, wouldn't you? Well, I'm not going to be that easy to get rid of."

"What I'd like to know is what you said to my sister. Are you going to tell me or not?"

"Not." Not waiting for a response to her refusal, she tucked her purse under her arm and marched out. When she reached the archway between the dining room and living room, she turned to glare at him. "Just in case I do buy this place, I'd appreciate it if you'd leave my house."

The front door slammed behind her. The boom echoed through the empty house ratcheting up Jason's blood pressure.

The woman drove him nuts.

Of course, Tammy Wright had her baby girl yesterday morning, and of course the news hit the paper today. The front page of the paper.

Right after the part where Cherry gave all the winnings from the baby pool to the Wrights to start a college fund for their new little girl, and right before the mention of Cherry's disappointment at being kept from the fair.

No less than four people stopped him to ask if he could do anything to help Lady Pandora get into the fair.

Then, to top it off, he arrived to pick up his daughter only to find Cherry, Lady Pandora herself, getting cozy with his sister.

So what if he'd been spoiling for a fight before he ever reached the house.

Hannah *was* fragile. She'd waited to start a family while she built her real estate business. But then Diane died, and as if she'd seen how precious time was, Hannah started talking babies. She'd been ecstatic when she learned she was pregnant. And devastated when she lost the baby.

Both times.

Loss had been too much a part of their lives the last three years.

He couldn't watch her go through that again. And he wouldn't allow Cherry Cooper to encourage her into experiencing that pain again.

Not that either of them appeared upset with the other. In fact, they'd been protective of each other, putting him in the hot seat when he'd only been trying to look out for his sister's best interests.

He'd never understand women. Hell, he barely understood himself these days. All he wanted was to maintain the status quo, raise his daughter, look out for his family, run his town.

Suddenly, life wasn't that simple. And it was all Cherry's fault. Not since he'd met Diane had he experienced such confusing emotions around a woman. He knew better than to let attraction rule him, to let longing fuel his blood. Hadn't he felt the pain of loss and how it tore a man apart?

He wanted the fortune teller gone. If she didn't leave town soon he'd likely do something rash.

Like pulling her into his arms and kissing those lush red lips.

Chapter Four

Walking back to her motel, her thoughts replaying the scene with Jason, Cherry hadn't gone far when she realized someone was following her. She sped up to see if she'd lost the person. The sense of being watched hadn't set off her usual triggers because she'd invited the limelight these last few days; consequently, people had been staring all morning.

This was different. This felt desperate. And by the sound of the accelerated footsteps, it was creeping up fast.

Cherry stopped and spun around. "Can I help you?"

"Oh." Her pursuer also stumbled to a halt. "I'm sorry."

A teenager, more child than woman but closing

the gap fast, stood on the sidewalk in dark, loose clothes. She probably meant the clothes to be slimming as she carried some extra weight, but they just looked hot. She'd pulled her dishwater blond hair into a ponytail except for two, long locks that fell over her eyes, a shield between her and the world.

It failed to hide the girl's despair and loneliness.

She looked ready to flee and though Cherry longed to put distance between her and the dictatorial mayor, her instinct to heal wouldn't let her disregard the obvious cry for help.

"It's okay," Cherry reassured her. "Did you want to ask me something?"

The girl wavered, clearly torn.

"You're Lady Pandora?" Her voice came out in little more than a whisper, as if she preferred not to draw attention to herself. "The lady who won the baby pool, who guessed the baby would be a girl?"

"Yes, I'm Lady Pandora." Cherry spoke softly to keep from scaring the girl away. She needed help; the sadness and anxiety in her reached for Cherry. "What's your name?"

"Melissa," the teenager answered, inching closer, and Cherry felt another heartbeat, another distressed soul. "Can you tell me if he's ever coming back? I just need to know if he's coming back?"

No need to ask who *he* was. This desperate half child was pregnant, the one she asked about was obviously the baby's father. The loose clothes and tentative manner took on a whole new light. She was hiding the pregnancy, which probably meant she hadn't seen a doctor.

Cherry longed to help Melissa, but she was under-age, immature and unprotected. Long ago, Cherry found out the hard way not to get involved in a situation like this. Her interference rarely helped matters and often made the circumstances worse.

"Melissa," she said softly. "I can't do a reading for you without your parents' permission. Is your mother around?"

Melissa's head went down and she started backing up.

"I have to go now."

"Wait." A lump formed in Cherry's throat, regret had her following the girl's retreat. "Melissa, you need to take care."

The girl wrapped her arms around herself and tucked her chin down. Her bowed head caused more strands of lank hair to fall in her face. The posture clearly confirmed her condition to someone who knew what to look for. Hugging herself, she turned to walk away.

"Melissa," Cherry put urgency in her voice. "You need to think of more than yourself right now. Have your mother take you to a doctor."

Sending a furtive glance over her shoulder, Melissa's gaze skittered away from Cherry's. "My mother's dead."

My mother's dead. The words rang in Cherry's head all night and into this morning. How sad, how desperate the girl who'd said the words. How lonely.

She'd made Cherry think of her own mother. Made her wonder about the woman who'd mistaken a cotton candy courtship for the real thing, who'd named her child after a city, who'd lived only long enough to see her baby born.

So here she stood, dawn barely coloring the morning sky, over her mother's grave.

Nona often mentioned Cherry's mother, little habits she'd had, similarities between her and Cherry, expressions they'd shared. And she'd never hesitated to answer Cherry's questions about her mother, but she never failed to cry when they talked in depth about her either. Even after all these years.

Today, Cherry carried a picture in her head of a woman young in years, old in spirit, friendly with all, reckless with one. Cherry would have liked to talk to her at least once.

Cherry knelt to clear fallen leaves and a few weeds from around the headstone, carefully placing a bouquet of daisies near the marble base.

Now, her father she had plenty of questions about. She had no point of reference for him except her dark hair, currently being teased by an early morning breeze, dark eyes and olive skin. The red in her hair came from her mother's side.

She'd resigned herself to the fact she'd never know more about her father.

Standing over her mother's grave, she felt sad to

have never met them—not deprived, because Nona took care of her too well for that. But she occasionally felt the sorrow for something she'd never had.

Just like she sometimes wished for the impossible—a stationary home, a career helping babies into the world, a family of her own. They all seemed beyond her reach.

At least she could see Nona settled in her own home. That in itself was a dream come true. Or would be when Jason Strong finally saw sense and stopped fighting her entrance to the fair.

A tingle on the back of her neck warned her. By thinking his name, she might well have conjured the man himself. She checked over her shoulder and, sure enough, he stood on the pathway about ten feet away, quietly waiting for her to finish her visit.

Standing, she faced him, her hands planted on her hips. "You're following me, aren't you?"

He removed a pair of sunglasses, tucked them in his suit pocket. "It's early. I saw your bike, thought I'd stop and check on you."

"Really?" More like check up on her. But she smiled, just to show him he couldn't get to her. "How thoughtful."

Rather than take issue, he gestured to the grave. "Your mother?"

Cherry hesitated, assessing him. Because his eyes held no rancor, she answered. "Yes. She died giving birth to me."

"I'm sorry for your loss. I know how difficult it is

for a girl to grow up without her mother. You're lucky you have your grandmother."

"Yes." She had been lucky. As he was raising a daughter on his own, she believed he understood how lucky. "I owe her a lot."

"My little girl is growing up without her mother. It's a hard rap."

Cherry remembered the bright, friendly, precocious little girl. Only a child well-loved showed that kind of openness and confidence.

"She has you. That counts for a lot."

"We stumble along okay, but sometimes I wonder if I'm cheating her because I'm not doing something I don't know to do. She was only a month old when my wife died. I don't want her missing out because of me."

"You have your mother, your sister. They'll help you. Rikki's sure to let you know what she wants." Like princess shoes and dress-up dolls. "You're way ahead of the game."

He grinned. "You're right. On all three counts. Still, I worry."

She narrowed the distance between them. "Good parents worry. I believe it's a prerequisite."

"I can attest to that."

Yeah, he understood. The fact he could admit to a weakness for his daughter touched her in unexpected ways. The little girl inside her that had never known her father melted at the concept of a man who cared enough to make himself vulnerable.

"They say you don't miss what you never had. I suppose that's true if you never knew it existed in the first place. But it's not true of parents. Nona is everything a mother could be to me and always has been. The love, attention, worry, guidance, discipline, it's mine unconditionally. But there's still a hole in my life because there's this person I never got to meet, to know, to love."

"Wow." He looked shell-shocked. "You can stop trying to make me feel better now."

She laughed as he'd meant her to. Poor Jason, he'd gotten more than he bargained for when he stopped to check on her.

She hooked her arm through his and turned him toward the street. His muscles flexed under her touch and even through the layers of his suit jacket and her leather, she felt his strength. She fought off the awareness of his sheer maleness.

"Relax. I didn't tell you this to freak you out."

"Too late."

"Wuss," she teased.

"When it comes to my daughter, you bet."

"I have a point to make."

"Whew. For a minute, I thought that was a sample of the advice you give out. It couldn't be good for business."

"Funny. But you're right, I do have advice. Don't be afraid to talk about Rikki's mother. Tell her stories, big things, little things. Habits. Likes. Dislikes. Don't force it. Just be natural. She may not understand now, but she'll remember when it matters."

"Your grandmother brought your mother to life for you."

"She did in so many ways. And I'm grateful for the knowledge. I'll never know my mom, but I know who she was. It's the best gift my grandmother ever gave me."

"I'll remember that."

"You should. It'll help you, too." She swept her free hand out, encompassing the cemetery with the gesture. "It's not necessary to say goodbye in order to let them go."

He immediately closed down. His expression, his eyes, his body language all turned flat. He pulled away from her. "I'm not a child. I don't need advice on how to cope."

"You're freaking out again. But there's no need to break a sweat. I'm not going hocus-pocus on you. In my business, I get a lot of people reaching out to the other side trying to find a way to say goodbye. I tell them death doesn't mean goodbye. You never lose the time you had with your loved one. You just have to stop letting sorrow rule your life."

He had no response for her, but she didn't expect one. The advice wasn't easy to hear. He'd need to reject it a few times before it took root.

"Anyway, thanks for checking on me." Stuffing her hands in her jacket pockets, she crossed the grass toward the street and her bike.

"Why are you looking for a house in my town?"

Cherry stopped. Sighed. Considered, then swung

to face him. "Buy me a cup of coffee at the BeeHive, and I'll tell you."

His long legs ate up the grass in half the time hers had. "I'll follow you."

Ten minutes later, she sat across from him in a window booth at the diner, steaming cups of coffee in front of them.

Jason sat quietly watching her, waiting for her to start. He had the patience of a very determined man. But then, she already knew that about him.

When he did speak, he surprised her with the question he asked. "How do you do it? How did you know my childhood nickname? How did you know Hannah was pregnant? That Tammy's baby would be a girl? How do you know?"

There he went again. Testing her. Since she had no answer he'd like or accept with alacrity, she didn't even try. "Magic."

His eyebrows lifted. "That's your answer? Magic?"

"Would you believe anything else?" she challenged.

"Try me," he offered.

She shrugged. "I really don't have any other explanation. Sometimes I just know things."

"That's it? You just know."

"Yeah. I've had the ability as long as I can remember. It would be like trying to explain how I breathe. So you see, it's easier to just say magic. I inherited my talent from my grandmother."

When he made no response, she realized there was no sense in delaying further. And no real reason why she shouldn't tell him her plans, except that knowledge was power. And he already held all the power. Maybe telling him about Nona would soften him up a bit. She hoped so.

"You asked about my grandmother. Where she was." She sipped the sweetened brew. "She's in a long-term facility in Lubbock. A year ago, she fell and broke her hip."

A frown drew his dark eyebrows together. "She still requires care after a year? What about surgery?"

"She's had three. And more complications than I have fingers." Tears welled up. She lowered her gaze to the depths of her coffee to keep him from noticing. "It's been a very difficult time."

She hated the idea of Nona suffering. She was so brave, so strong. She never gave up trying, never gave up faith she'd walk again as well as before. Every day she came closer to reaching her goal, but it was a long, painful trial.

And Cherry couldn't even be there to help her through the agony of it.

"I imagine it is for a woman who's spent the better part of her life on the open road."

"According to her doctor, she won't be doing any more trips on the road. She'll walk, she's bound and determined to be mobile. But she'll never have the agility she had before. She's in her seventies. She says it's time she had a home of her own. And I'm going to see she gets it."

"I see. And she's chosen to make her home in Blossom City?"

"Her daughter is buried here. So, yes, this is where she wants to live."

A waitress came by, filled their cups, moved away. Cherry used the moment to gather her composure. Sharing her troubles didn't come easily to her.

"And you?" he asked.

"Me?" Confused she raised her eyes to his. "What about me?"

"Will you be making your home in Blossom as well?" He kept his tone and expression carefully bland.

Smart man. But he didn't fool her. No way he wanted her hanging around his town.

"Don't worry, Mayor. I won't be moving in with Nona. Someone has to pay the mortgage, which means I'll be on the road doing the circuit."

Funny, he didn't look as relieved by the news as she would have thought. Because she didn't understand the way that made her feel, she traced a finger around the rim of her mug.

"Now you know why it's so important for me to get into the fair. Nona's medical expenses have taken a bite out of our savings. I need the income from this run to get the house."

With a sigh, she laid her hands flat on the table, a symbol of sorts; she'd laid all her cards out for him to see. Now she relied on his sense of fair play and decency to do the right thing.

Jason set his hands on the table, close but not quite

touching hers. He wanted to bridge the distance, to feel the softness of her skin, to offer comfort.

He fought the urge because no good could come from his attraction to her.

"What happens if you don't get the money?" he asked. Not because he wasn't sympathetic, not even because he didn't believe in her talents—the Lord knew she'd given him enough food for thought there—but because no matter how much he'd like to help her, his obligations to his people came first.

Disappointment flickered in her exotic eyes, but she didn't back down. "Then Nona stays in long-term care and our plans are delayed by a year, maybe eighteen months. This is fair season, we make half our yearly income during the summer months. With the additional cost of Nona's care, it'll take me that long to earn the extra reserves needed. And then we'll be back."

"But it wouldn't change your long-term plans?"

"No. This is where my mother's buried, so this is where Nona wants to live. She's given me everything I've ever needed. And this is all she's ever asked for in return. I'm going to see she gets it."

"Even if it takes you a year? Wouldn't it be easier to rent an apartment for her in Lubbock?"

She shrugged. "Easier. But it's not what she wants. Keeping me from the fair won't keep us out of Blossom. It'll just delay the inevitable, and Nona will be the one to suffer."

All earnest concern, she leant forward affording

him a grand view of creamy cleavage. "You don't want to make an old lady suffer, do you Jason?"

"No, of course not." He swallowed hard, then again when the sweet scent of woman reached him. He sat back in sheer self-defense.

"Unfortunately, it's not that clear-cut. This town has suffered, too. We're just beginning to recover. No matter how sympathetic I am to your cause or how the public has responded to your sensationalism, I have to think of the town first. Your presence in the fair could undo all the good we've accomplished in the last two years."

"I know about the Swindle. I'm sorry the town suffered because of an unscrupulous fortune-teller, but that's not who I am. My grandmother is going to live here. I can promise you I won't be doing anything to cause her trouble with the townspeople."

From her expression, he knew she considered the promise her ace in the hole. And it did say a lot. But he realized he wasn't totally impartial when it came to the lovely Lady Pandora. Best if he waited for Trace's final report.

"I'm not sure I can take that chance."

Rather than the disappointment he expected to see, she blasted him with a bright smile. "You thought about it. I'll take that. It's the closest I've gotten so far."

Her optimism blew him away. "Don't get your hopes up." He warned. "I'm probably not going to change my mind."

She actually laughed. "Hey, don't spoil the moment. In fact, I'm so excited I'm willing to share what Rikki wants for her birthday."

His suspicions rose, but she rolled her eyes at him.

"Please, the child doesn't know a stranger, she told me what she wants."

That was his girl. "I have the list, thanks. A Barbie, a doll that walks and talks, a pony, coloring books, a new dress and a baby brother."

She bit her lip to keep a straight face. "I guess I can't help with that list."

He sent her a wry glance. "I've already prepared her for disappointment regarding the last."

"Ah." She nodded sagely. "I was talking about the pony."

The outrageous comment surprised a laugh from him. She had a way of doing that that completely disarmed him.

"Princess shoes," she said, throwing him yet again.

"Princess what?" He felt foolish just voicing the question.

"Shoes. Rikki wants princess shoes for her birthday."

"Princess shoes." Jason repeated. He had no clue what that meant and he had no intention of asking. This woman already had him twisted in knots. He didn't dare give her any more of an edge. "Thanks."

Chapter Five

Friday finally dawned and with it the arrival of the carnies. Cherry waited on a fence rail across from the rodeo arena, watching people come and go as things geared up for the Stampede later today. Along with a chili cook-off and concert series, the Stampede was the official launch of the rodeo, which started tomorrow.

She might mosey over later and try some chili. In the meantime, the caravan should be here any time. Carlo had called to say they'd be here at two. They had the weekend to set up, with the fair starting on Tuesday.

Out by the road, picketers carried signs protesting the carnival. Protesting her.

She longed to see her friends, to talk to someone who neither wanted nor expected anything from her.

Someone who didn't look at her with hope, desperation or suspicion. Someone who treated her as an equal.

Being "on" all day, every day, took a lot out of a person. A professional, she knew how to play to her audience. She wore the bright colors, silk scarves, long flowing skirts and peasant tops people associated with gypsies and fortune-tellers.

These last few days, she'd played the part to the hilt and strained her talent to the max. Yet it might have all been for nothing.

She dialed Nona's number, smiled when her grandmother came on the line. "Hey tinsel toes, I hear rumors you'll be dancing at my wedding."

A delighted laugh sounded down the line. "As long as you don't get married for a few months. Oh Cherry, for the first time I feel like I'll have a life again. It's so good to move without pain, I'm ready to get up and dance right now."

"Nona, Nona, Nona." God, the woman had more gumption than someone half her age. Cherry loved her to death. "Promise me you'll follow the doctor's orders."

"Promises, promises. How are things going in Blossom? Has the mayor accepted the inevitable yet?"

"Nothing is inevitable, you taught me that. Lot of good being a psychic is doing me. I can't read Jason for nothing. Half the time, I think he wants to help me." She saw it in his eyes. "The other half, he's ready to run me out of town on a rail to protect his precious town."

"Cherry."

"Which, as well as being highly annoying, is totally admirable."

"You like him," Nona said.

She did. Damn it.

God, he was a gorgeous piece of work, on the inside as well as the outside. The longer she stayed in town, the more dangerous he became.

"He makes me long for things I can't have."

"Like a permanent home? A respected career? A family of your own? You're the only one stopping yourself from having those things."

"I have to stay on the road, or we won't be able to afford the house."

"Dear, I can't stay in the house if it means you're not happy."

"Nona, don't say that. This is what you want, what you need, what you deserve. My turn will come. It's just not here and now."

"And what about the mayor?"

"The mayor will come through. If I have to seduce him, then blackmail him, he'll come through."

Again Nona laughed. "Sounds like a plan."

"Remember the Swindle that had the city council up in arms, and how it was the reason I was being kept out of the fair? Well, there's this whole concerned citizens' group that's made it their mission to keep the town from a repeat performance. It's called the Committee for Moral Behavior."

"Has anyone given you a bad time?" Concern replaced all levity in Nona's voice.

"No, not so far. A few dirty looks, a couple of shouted insults."

"Sounds like the same suspicion we usually get as outsiders."

"Mostly, yeah. Except this committee doesn't want the carnival in town at all." She shaded her eyes to see the main gate. "There's a picket line of protesters at the front gate and the carnival workers aren't even here yet."

"Oh my. I don't like it that you're there alone. When do you expect Carlo and the rest of the caravan?"

Cherry checked her watch. You could set your clock by Carlo's schedule. "They should be here in the next half hour, maybe sooner."

"Good. What's your mayor doing about this extremist group?"

"Nona, they're concerned citizens, not extremists. And he's not *my* mayor. But I understand now why he's being so cautious. It's a small but vocal group. And led by several prominent citizens."

"Defending the mayor. Now that's interesting." Nona didn't linger over the notion, though Cherry knew she'd ponder it in depth once they were off the phone. Now she went back to the topic under discussion. "What do your senses tell you?"

Cherry chose her words carefully. She didn't want to lie to her grandmother, but the truth—that her senses failed to tell her anything—would only upset Nona.

"I don't need to use my talents to know there's still healing to be done here. Don't get me wrong. You're going to like Blossom City. For the most part, the people are friendly, if a little eccentric." She grinned, thinking it was time to lighten the mood. "You can get that tattoo you're always threatening to get at the Cut N Curl."

"I am not getting a tattoo." Her voice lowered on the last word. "Shame on you for teasing an old, sick woman."

Cherry rolled her eyes. "Oh come on, you know you want one just like mine."

"Wicked child."

A low, male rumble sounded on Nona's end of the line followed by Nona's delighted giggle. "Oh hush. I'm on the phone with my granddaughter."

"Oh ho." Cherry drew out the vowels. "You've met someone, haven't you?" She deliberately fed Nona's words back to her. "A man."

"Now don't you start. I'm too old for such nonsense. And I know when I'm being distracted."

"Yeah? So do I. I want to hear all the details."

"Here comes the nurse with my afternoon meds. I'm going to have to go."

Cherry laughed. "Coward."

"I'll talk to you tomorrow."

"Nona." Cherry caught her before she disconnected. "Beware Prince Charming."

"Brat." With a click, she was gone.

"You bet you'll talk to me tomorrow." Cherry said

to herself. For all her teasing, she fully intended finding out all the details about the mysterious man in Nona's life.

A white Lexus pulled up next to the fence where Cherry sat. Hannah Brown sat behind the wheel and Rikki Strong waved to Cherry from the back passenger seat.

Hannah's brow furrowed in a frown matching the look of harassment laced with anxiety in her eyes.

Cherry hopped down and went to the Lexus, leaning down to wave at Rikki. "Hey, you girls out for ride?"

"I'm running late," Hannah said. "I'm supposed to drop Rikki off with Jason, but he wasn't at his office like he said he'd be. They said he was over at the big barn in the veterinarian's office. Do you know which one is the big barn?"

"Sure." Cherry shaded her eyes to focus on the half-dozen buildings housing the livestock and rodeo animals. She pointed. "It's behind those first two smaller barns and to the left. I don't know where the vet's office is, though."

"Darn. I tried calling his cell but he's not answering. I'm already going to be late for my doctor's appointment."

"Ah." That explained the anxiousness. "I'll take her for you." Cherry made the offer even though Hannah probably wouldn't take her up on it. Yes, they'd taken to each other, but Hannah didn't really know Cherry well enough to trust the little girl to her care without her brother's permission. Even as Cherry saw the regret in Hannah's expression, her cell phone rang.

"Where are you? I don't have time to be running all over the fairgrounds." Hannah's nervousness showed in a flare of temper as she let her brother have it for not being where he said he'd be. "I have to go. Cherry's going to walk Rikki over to you. Right. I'll tell her."

She disconnected and gave Cherry a grateful smile. "Thanks for helping out. Jason's going to walk out to meet you. He said to tell you he has news for you." Hannah climbed from the car, and Cherry joined her in walking around to the back where Rikki was strapped into her child's seat. Hannah explained to the little girl that Cherry would walk her over to her daddy by the barns.

Not a shy bone in her body, Rikki cheerfully wiggled out of her seat and hopped down to grab Cherry's hand.

"Do you think we'll see some kittens?"

"Kittens?" Cherry looked to Hannah. Did Blossom County have a category for kittens in their fair?

Hannah shook her head. "Her friend's cat had kittens in a barn." She reclaimed her seat behind the wheel, started the car. "Thanks," she called as she pulled onto the road with a small cloud of dirt.

Cherry glanced down at Rikki to find the child looking up at her expectantly. Ah, yes, kittens. "I don't think there are any kittens, but there's probably some bunnies. And Betsy, the three-legged pig."

Enthralled by the notion of a handicapped pig, Rikki bombarded Cherry with questions as they walked along the outside of the rodeo arena and headed for the barns. It wasn't long, however, before Rikki moved on to her favorite topic: a reminder of her upcoming birthday and an in-depth description of the princess shoes she wanted.

"I had high heels when I was a little girl," Cherry confessed, "but they didn't have the poufy feathers. Cool."

"Cool." Rikki grinned. "You can comed to my party. It's Sataday." She started in on a list of people coming to her party.

Cherry only half listened to the list of names. Down the way, she saw Jason coming toward them.

Tall and broad, he filled out the jeans and black T-shirt he wore to perfection. A cream-colored Stetson covered his dark hair. Seeing him in the casual clothes, how they clung and defined the muscles in his arms and legs, reminded Cherry of her first impression of him as a warrior. He certainly blended with the macho, rugged cowboys as if he belonged.

The man needed some warts. Or a paunch. Maybe some thinning hair. Anything to put her off. All that decency wrapped up in a to-die-for package made the man very hard to resist.

The little bundle of energy walking beside her only added to his appeal.

"...Abe is mad at his mom cause she was bad."

Rikki's comment drew Cherry's attention from

father to daughter. Cherry frowned, distressed at the thought of Rikki's friend in a bad situation.

As an outsider, she'd learned to mind her own counsel when it came to interfering in the lives of the townspeople. Sure, they wanted their fortunes read, but that didn't give her license to butt into their business.

But she couldn't turn a blind eye to a child in an abusive situation. Questioning Rikki went against the grain, but kids often saw what adults overlooked.

"Has Abe's mom ever hurt him?" Cherry gently probed. At the same time, she opened her senses seeking a path to the boy through the girl.

The first thing she felt was the overwhelming love surrounding the girl. Her confidence and joy in life came directly from that core of love.

One more admirable quality to add to Jason's list.

Rikki looked up at Cherry as if surprised by her question. "No silly. She was a bad girl."

"Oh, right." Cherry narrowed in on the path between girl and boy. Not an easy task, as this wasn't her true talent. Concentrating hard, she absorbed confusion and disappointment but no element of violence or pain. "Silly."

"Should I tell Daddy?" For the first time, Cherry heard uncertainty in the child's voice, clearly torn by divided loyalties.

"I think you can tell your daddy anything." Cherry had no doubt that would always be true. Neither did she doubt the girl would put it to the test over the years.

"Yeah. He's really smart." A huge grin broke over the angelic face. "And brave. Like Prince Charming."

Cherry flinched at the royal reference. If she believed in signs, that would definitely qualify as a tell. Good thing Nona wasn't here to remind her of the power of signs.

"There's Daddy." Rikki broke away from Cherry to race to her father. Jason bent down and swept his daughter into his arms, lifting her high against his shoulder. The intimacy of the union between them brought a knot of emotion to Cherry's throat.

No matter how much she denied it to Nona, to her carny friends, to herself—she wanted moments like this that belonged to her. She wanted the man, the child, the love.

It was almost too beautiful to watch.

From ten feet away, Cherry heard Rikki demanding to see Betsy, the three-legged pig. Jason responded, his voice a deep murmur in contrast to Rikki's excited chatter.

Not wanting to intrude, Cherry stopped short, waiting for Jason to look up so she could acknowledge Rikki's safe delivery and make her escape.

As if reading her mind, he glanced up and caught her gaze, his eyes eating her up in one heated sweep from head to foot. It seemed he enjoyed the look of her in her jeans as much as she liked the look of him in his.

But he only said, "Hey."

"Hey." So much for scintillating conversation.

Still, his eyes said more than enough. More than either of them dared say aloud. She cocked a hip, tucked a thumb in a belt loop and nodded toward Rikki. "Sign, sealed, and delivered."

"Thanks. There was a bit of an emergency. I know Hannah appreciated your help."

"No problem." Cherry shrugged away the gratitude as she backed away, feeling the need for distance between them. "I'll see you around. Bye, Rikki."

Spinning on her heel, she headed back the way she'd come.

"Wait, Don't you want to hear the news I have for you?"

"Right." He had news. Lord, she hoped he was ready to let her into the fair. Then she could submerge back into her world and forget he existed.

"Daddy, the piggy."

"Rikki," he admonished gently, "I'm talking to Cherry."

"But I wanna see the piggy. Cherry see the piggy, too." Rikki played her daddy like a finely tuned violin.

"Really?" Jason lifted a brow, the look in his eyes letting her know that though he indulged his daughter he was very much the maestro in charge. "Shall we view the piggy?"

"Why not?" Cherry fell into step with him.

He set Rikki on her feet and she ran ahead. He called out, "Stay where I can see you."

"She's going to be a handful when she gets older."

He cringed. "You have no idea how much the thought terrifies me."

Cherry laughed at the exaggerated fear in his voice. "You're safe for a few years yet. She still thinks you're Prince Charming."

"Really?" He grinned, obviously delighted by the revelation.

Silently, Cherry sighed. What did you do with a man clearly besotted with his daughter, who showed such pleasure in being considered her hero?

Maybe stop fighting the inevitable and give into the attraction? Possibly have a full-fledged cotton candy courtship?

"So what's this news you have for me?"

His smile stayed in place. "What, you can't read my mind?"

"Oh, so you want to play?" She slowed, then stopped. "Reading minds isn't really one of my talents." Planting her hands on her hips, she met him challenge for challenge. "But I'm willing to give it a try if you're willing to chance it."

Desire lit up his eyes. He took a step forward, the warrior in him not a bit afraid of the dare in her posture. But rather than act on the chemistry arcing in the air, he stopped and looked around at all the activity. When he turned those blue-gray eyes back on her, the burning passion had been banked and the mayor once more held control, the status quo reestablished.

Though he made no move to retreat, he shoved his

hands in his pockets and announced. "After due consideration, I've decided to let you perform at the fair."

"Really?" A grin bubbled up, satisfaction her first reaction.

Finally! She celebrated with a shimmy dance not even caring that His Honor watched.

For all her bravado these last few days, she hadn't truly known he'd come through with authorization. When it came to this town, his protective streak was a mile wide.

She halted midshimmy, suddenly unwilling to cause him trouble. "What about the Committee for Moral Behavior? They won't be thrilled with your decision."

His eyebrows lifted. "What do you know of the CMB? Have you had a run-in with someone?"

"Not exactly a run-in," she denied with a wry smile. "Bitsy Dupres gently advised me a fortune-teller was not welcome in town."

He shrugged off the warning. "Bitsy means well, but the CMB is a small group with more time than sense. For the most part, they're harmless. The sheriff has given his approval after an extensive security investigation. So, yeah, you're in the fair. But I'm going to ask you not to dispense financial advice."

"I promise." Thrilled to have the go-ahead, Cherry ignored the reference to a security investigation and launched herself at Jason, hugging him. "Thank you," she chimed before planting a kiss on his cheek.

Skin touched skin. And pow. In an instant, life

changed forever. She felt his heat, his muscles coil as he braced his body, then the scent of him—traces of sweat, soap, and man. Her lips against his cheek, the softness of skin, the harshness of bristles.

The reality of love.

Her system absorbed the shock even as her mind opened and her senses flared. She knew, just knew, in that moment that this man, this near stranger, was her soul mate.

Fear and denial rose up fast and hard.

Oh, no. No. No!

Slowly, she backed away. This couldn't be, wouldn't be.

"Cherry?" Slate-blue eyes narrowed on her. Jason's one step forward swallowed two of hers in retreat. "What is it?"

"Nothing." She mouthed the word, but nothing made it past the lump constricting her throat. So it had happened to her grandmother. One touch with grandpa, and she'd fallen like a star from the sky.

"You've gone white. Talk to me." The demand held the bite of concern.

"I…ah…" Cherry continued to backpedal. "Gotta go."

She turned and ran, uncaring of who saw or what impression she left behind her. She was running for her life.

Chapter Six

Jason watched Cherry dodge between two of the smaller barns.

What just happened here?

He'd never seen her anything but calm and collected. Or downright feisty. But he'd just seen full-blown panic in her eyes. Something was wrong, real wrong.

He meant to find out what.

Looking around for Rikki, he found her talking to Cindy Tucker, a friend and neighbor.

"Cindy," he called. The young redhead glanced up. "Can you watch Rikki for a few minutes?"

She nodded and waved, acknowledging his request.

Satisfied, Jason took off after Cherry. He followed her through the gap in buildings, saw her turn to the left when she reached the end. A few minutes later, he caught up to her on the far side of the big barn. All the activity was at the front of the barns, so no one was back here.

She stood slumped against the building, her arms crossed protectively over her chest.

Not wanting to spook her, he approached slowly, stopping when her bowed head almost touched his chest.

"Cherry?" A hand under her chin lifted her gaze to his. "Are you okay?"

"Yes. No." She pulled away, put additional inches between them. "I don't know."

His gut clenched at the sight of her bittersweet chocolate eyes misted with tears. "What's the matter? What happened back there?"

Distress wrinkled her delicate brow and even, white teeth worried her full bottom lip. A sign of her uncertainty. "My world just turned upside down."

"You're not making sense." He shook his head, hating the helplessness that accompanied lack of understanding.

"You're right. It makes no sense."

She began to pace, mumbling to herself. "Maybe I imagined it. You're a gorgeous guy. Of course, I'm attracted to you. And you to me. Chemistry. That's all it is. No big deal. Just a natural reaction to—"

"Cherry," he clasped her elbow, swung her around. She came to a stop, her hands resting on his forearms. "You're beginning to worry me."

Gently he lifted her chin. Blinking, she focused on

him. Emotions—hope, despair, fear, longing—roiled in the brown depths of her eyes. And he saw a sudden desperate resolve before she rose on her toes and threw her arms around his neck. Her eyes closed just as her lips landed on his.

He didn't see anything after that. His eyes closed, too, and he stopped thinking to feel.

Oh, he'd wanted this, to taste her, to gather her warmth next to his body and just absorb her joy for life. Her mouth opened under his and he sank into the heat. She welcomed him with a dance of tongues, rising further up on her toes to press her breasts into his chest. Her flavor, sweet as the chocolate of her eyes, intoxicated him, making him forget everything but how right she felt in his arms.

Lifting her off her feet and back against the barn, he sank deeper into her, demanding she give all to the insanity she'd started, giving his all in the passionate exchange.

The need for air didn't stop them, but the intrusion of voices nearby did.

Pulling his mouth free, he quickly stepped back. Without him to hold her up, Cherry teetered, swaying as if dizzy. He caught her by the elbows and held her steady.

As soon as she had her balance, Cherry pulled free of Jason. She'd hoped by kissing him, she'd prove her premonition wrong.

She should have known better.

Instead of proving the opposite, she proved the accuracy of her touch. Jason Strong felt right, tasted right, fit right. Everything about him thrilled her. When they touched, she felt the zing from toenails to hair follicles, and everywhere in between.

But he couldn't be more wrong for her.

He was grounded, with generations of family behind him. She was four wheels, on the go, with one person in the world she belonged to.

They couldn't be more different.

She backed up, came up hard against the side of the barn and gladly accepted the support for her shaky knees.

"Okay, that was a bad idea." Pushing the hair out of her face, she effectively avoided his eyes. Feeling like a fool and having it confirmed were two different things. She couldn't bear to see regret in Jason's expression.

"Bad never tasted so good." Far from showing regret, he cupped her elbow and led her further down the length of the barn away from the sounds of activity and the off chance of someone glancing around the corner and seeing the mayor in a lurid embrace.

The thought should shock some sense into her, but his touch offset normal thought.

They had this moment; she meant to steal as much from it as possible.

Jason crowded close again. "I think I'm addicted."

"Hmm." Relief joined the desire already bubbling through her system making her light-headed. "Me, too. Too bad it can't happen again."

"Yeah." He rested his forehead against hers; his hat pushed back shading them both. "Too bad."

"So you agree there's no future to this?" She closed her eyes, savored his closeness.

He sighed. "Hell, I don't even know what this is."

She laughed. "An aberration?"

"I guess that works as good as anything." His warm breath bathed her cheek, melted her insides.

"That's the problem. This isn't going to work at all. Unless you're up for a summer fling?"

Unable to resist, she turned toward his mouth, lips seeking lips, brushing once, twice. Knowing she only prolonged the separation, she tried to stop, but he followed and deepened the kiss, taking them once more on a sensual journey.

The need for air finally brought them to the surface. Jason threaded his fingers through her hair, tilting her head back so she met his blue-gray gaze. "Short-term isn't my style, and I don't think it's your style either."

"Not usually." She bit her lip, surprised at her bold proposition. Yet willing to make an exception to explore this emotional anomaly. "But I've never felt this way before. We call them cotton candy courtships."

His dark eyebrows lifted and his eyes narrowed even as a possessiveness entered the gray depths. "You have a name for summer flings?"

She nodded, secretly pleased by his show of jealousy. "A cotton candy courtship—full of fluff, little substance, but sweet while it lasts."

"I see. And how often have you indulged in a cotton candy courtship?"

"Once or twice. Years ago, when I was young and foolish. Even knowing it was going to end after a few weeks didn't prevent the pain of splitting up."

He relaxed slightly, brushed back a curl that persisted in falling into her eyes. "If it were just me—I'm the mayor, I have to think of more than myself. Especially with the Committee for Moral Behavior kicking up a fuss over the whole carnival thing."

"I thought you said the CMB was harmless."

"For the most part. The mayor indulging in an affair with the fortune-teller from the carnival would generate enough gossip to boost their power. My family's been around for generations. We built this town. I can weather the storm. You and your friends in the carnival would take the brunt of their spleen."

"I see." She barely kept from flinching at his description of their fictitious relationship. But if he could think of her before himself, she could think of her carny friends before herself. Especially when they both agreed there was no future for a relationship between them.

"So we're agreed, this can't happen again."

"It's for the best."

"Right," Cherry said, trying to keep the sadness from her voice.

Not quite ready to let him go, she laid her head on his shoulder, savoring the rightness and comfort of being in his arms, resigning herself to the fact she'd never experience the feeling again. She listened to the steady, slightly rapid beat of his heart. Her cowboy was not unaffected.

Too bad he took his responsibilities so seriously.

Of course if he didn't, he wouldn't be the man she believed him to be.

"Where's Rikki?"

"With a friend. I should get back to her."

"Yes."

Neither moved away from the other; instead, they clung together. Cherry tightened her arms around Jason's waist, knowing she should let go but unable to make the first move.

"You leave first." She whispered the words.

"No, you leave first." He rubbed his chin over the top of her head. The huskiness in his voice sent a responding shiver through her. He wasn't finding this any easier than she was. "I haven't felt this aroused or at peace since my wife died."

An odd combination, but she knew exactly what he meant. "Did you find the ring?"

His arms tightened. "Yes. I'm not even going to ask how you did that." A moment of silence passed. "Thank you."

"You're welcome." She smiled and turned her head to place a kiss over his heart. For a nonbeliever, he displayed amazing acceptance.

He shifted, lowering his hands to squeeze her butt, lifting her against him so she felt the full effect she had on him.

She gasped and her gaze flew up to meet his. "What are you doing? I thought we were trying to cool down here."

"You have a fantastic butt. I especially like it in black leather. I couldn't get this close and not touch." He squeezed again. "Hmm. Blue denim isn't bad, either. It's almost enough to make me change my mind. I'll never look at cotton candy again without thinking of you."

"I hope it makes you sweat."

He grinned and kneaded. "Have no doubt."

Unable to resist, she wiggled her hips against him and watched his eyes roll up in his head before the lids closed.

He groaned. "That's why you have to leave first. I have a physical handicap."

"No fair. Just because I don't have body parts poking out doesn't mean I'm in any better shape than you."

He threw back his head and roared. "Damn, you make me laugh. I can't remember when I've had a better time."

"You find frustration fun, do you?" She loved the sound of his laughter, felt it had been missing in his life these last few years.

"The frustration is worth this." He cradled her face in gentle hands and adored her with his mouth. She felt both ravished and cherished at the same time. It took all her strength not to cling when he lifted his head, tipped his hat at her and walked away.

* * *

While occupied with Jason, Cherry missed the arrival of the carnival caravan. She found Carlo directing the carnies to the camping sites that would be their homes for the next four weeks.

Her rig was already set up on the edge of the back pasture adjacent to the fairgrounds allocated to them by the city for use during the run of the fair.

"Carlo." She threw herself into the arms of her dark haired, silver-eyed friend, waiting for the feeling of home to overcome her. When it didn't, she realized she'd left the feeling behind the back side of the barn in the arms of a future she'd never see. "I'm so glad you finally got here."

"Hey now, gypsy girl, there you are." Carlo hugged her closely, then released her to direct the next rig into an open spot. "I expected you to be waiting at the gate for us."

"Yeah. Well, something came up." Cherry almost wished she'd stayed seated on the fence. Almost. "It's good to see you guys."

Carlo fished in his pants pocket, then tossed her her keys. "How have the good folks of Blossom been treating you? Am I going to have to take on the mayor or did he see reason?"

"I'm in." She grinned and slapped palms with him in a high-five salute. "He just gave me the news. I think it was the legal research we did on the Internet that swayed him to my side."

White teeth flashed against his olive skin, crinkling the edges of the scar on the right side of his face. "If that were the case, you'd have been in days ago."

"Maybe so." Cherry didn't completely dismiss his help. Jason respected the law, and she knew she'd made an impression with the information they'd dug up. "But it didn't hurt. And I really appreciate your help. With everything."

A horn honked, Cherry looked up to find two friends waving frantically. The twins, Jan and Marie, were belly dancers with the troupe. If Cherry hadn't been able to convince Jason to let her in as a fortune-teller, her friends had invited her to join them in their exotic show.

Cherry was glad not to have to take them up on their offer. Not only wouldn't she make the money she needed, but give her a crystal ball over belly button baubles any day.

"No sweat, gypsy girl." Carlo waved off her gratitude. "Now get out of here before you get run over."

Cherry gratefully went to reclaim her home.

"Jason, I can't believe you let the fortune-teller into the fair." Cassie Twain stormed into his office.

Cassie had become Hannah's real estate partner a year after Diane died. A no-nonsense business-woman, she wore conservative suits in conservative colors, which matched her nondescript brown hair worn in an unimaginative bob.

They shared a three-office suite in a building on the town square. He tried to get by his office here two or three times a week, but most the time he ended up taking work home or with him to the mayor's office.

He leaned back in his leather chair and gave the slim brunette his full attention. She waved off his offer of a seat to pace the office with nervous energy.

"Cassie, it's city business. I'm sorry if the Committee for Moral Behavior doesn't approve, but I have to do what I feel is best."

"How can it be best to let another fortune-teller loose on the citizens of Blossom? Don't you remember how many people suffered the last time?"

"Yes. It was rough and I know you don't want to hear this, but I can no longer let the loss of a few affect the economy of the entire town."

"You already contracted with the carnival. Surely there was no need to allow the fortune-teller in as well." Cassie's agitation increased as she spoke of the carnival, not surprising since she and her husband Fred had been victims of the Swindle. "Wouldn't it be better to do this one step at a time?"

"Perhaps. But it wasn't worth the legal risk to the city to keep her out. Her contract with the carnival troupe preceded the troupe's contract with the city. It could be argued the troupe had no right to sign away her right to perform."

"She has no right to do anything in this town," Cassie snapped. "You need to tell her you changed your mind again and she should leave."

Jason stood and rounded the desk, using the time to harness his impatience. Cassie'd never been one of his favorite people. He accepted her for his sister's sake. For Hannah, he tolerated the woman in his business and social life, but nobody told him how to run his town.

"You suffered a loss. I sympathize." And he did. He sympathized, but he didn't understand. Cassie was a real estate agent, she should have known the con man's land offer was too good to be true.

"A lot of people suffered losses, prominent people who aren't going to be happy to hear of your decision. People like the Clarks, the Cahills, the Dupres."

"Okay that's enough." Jason's patience had just run out. "For one thing, the Dupres were not victims of the Swindle. For another, you need to get hold of yourself. The decision was made with the full support of the city council, and it stands."

Cassie flinched. Her head and shoulders went back, her mouth tightened and rage flared in her narrowed eyes. Abruptly, she turned away and wrapped her arms around herself.

Jason's hackles rose. Her reaction seemed out of proportion to the situation. When she faced him a moment later, she had regained her normal staunch demeanor.

"Of course, you're right," she said quietly. "I was confused for a moment. Bitsy once told me she almost invested in the project. Lucky for her, she didn't. Perhaps I am taking this too personally, but for me it is."

Now his senses went on red alert. He'd never known Cassie to admit to a failing, to being wrong or simply confused. She always had an out or refused to accept the blame.

"No one expects you to be objective, Cassie, but it is expected of me. I have to look at the bigger picture. It's up to me to see Blossom's economy doesn't continue to decline because of something that happened two years ago."

"But the fortune-teller—"

"Cherry Cooper is not going to rook anyone." Jason heard the harshness of his tone and forced himself to take a calming breath. "Trace has done an extensive security check on her. Her reputation is impeccable. She and her grandmother have worked with several law enforcement agencies in recovering missing people."

"I see." Cassie's tone suggested she saw more than he'd meant to reveal.

Perhaps he'd defended Cherry more than discretion warranted, but he refused to sit still in the face of ignorant generalizations. He conveniently chose to forget he'd been guilty of the same just a week ago.

"We've taken every precaution to make sure a swindle doesn't happen again. That's the best I can do."

"I hope you're ready for a fight, Jason." Her chin went up and her expression took on a superior smirk. "The CMB believes there are ways to bring income into the county without attracting a bad element with it."

His patience at an end, Jason returned to his seat

behind the desk and picked up his pen. "We're a wet county surrounded by dry counties. People come from at least six counties for the alcohol and amusement rides. You're not going to generate the same kind of revenue with a bake sale."

He didn't bother to look up when she gasped her outrage and slammed out of the office.

Chapter Seven

Cherry donned jeans and a white peasant shirt and threaded a shimmering purple scarf through the belt loops. It felt good to be back in her trailer, back among her things, her friends.

Yet after only a day, she missed Jason.

She tidied her breakfast dishes, slipped on her sneakers and headed for her tent on the midway. Made of red canvas, it was six by eight feet and seven feet high. Last night, she'd pitched the tent and moved over the tables and chairs she used. Today, she'd place the furniture and decorate with posters and scarves. Her crystal ball she carried back and forth.

By midmorning, she had the lunar and tarot posters in place and scarves draped artistically along the back and sides to create a mystical atmosphere. She tied back the two front flaps, then fed two sheer gold panels on to a curtain rod.

Working from the middle, she attempted to lodge the rod into the upper front corners. For some reason, the left side refused to catch. She shifted and shoved to no avail. Mumbling unmentionable words under her breath, she rose on her toes and pushed hard. And would have fallen except hard arms caught her around the waist.

She twisted to look up into Jason's blue-gray eyes. "Hello."

"Hey." He set her on her feet. "Looks like you need help."

Tugging her shirt into place, she eyed his six-foot-plus frame with appreciation. In khaki pants and a short-sleeved white polo shirt, he looked cool and collected. And just what she needed.

"From a handsome man with a long reach? Oh yeah." She picked up the rod. "Grab that end. It goes as high into that corner as you can get."

He went to his corner and she took the other end, but it still wouldn't fit. She met his gaze across the short distance. "The two halves must have come unclicked."

"I'll fix it." He found the middle, made the adjustment and a moment later they had the rod in place. The sheer gold panels flowed to the ground, casting the tent into a gilded haven of privacy.

"What are you doing here?" Tempted by his unexpected closeness but conscious of their agreement to keep to their own worlds, she stuffed her hands into her back pockets and rocked on her heels.

He pulled his gaze from an inspection of the tent to focus on her. "I need your help."

"Oh?"

Hands at his waist, he raked her with a look that meant trouble, pure and simple. His slow grin held a sheepish quality. "Exactly what are princess shoes?"

Her insides melted and her will weakened.

Not good. Not good at all. She'd missed him, yeah, but with cooler hormones and a clear head, she saw the wisdom of staying on her side of the ticket booth.

Yet how did she deny a father's plea? And really, what harm was there in spending a few minutes in his company?

"Princess shoes are little girl high heels decorated with feathers or fake gems."

He looked truly appalled. "Tell me you're kidding."

She laughed, enjoying his dismay. "Nope. They're truly gaudy, but to a three-year old they're beautiful. In fact, the gaudier the better."

Jason hung his head and shook it sadly. But he recovered quickly lifting his head and bracing his shoulders. "A father's got to do what a father's got to do."

"You'll be her hero."

"Yeah, that'll help when I'm wandering through the frou-frou department."

Biting off a laugh, she said, "You are such a guy."

His chest puffed up, and he flexed a few muscles. "Have no doubt."

Oh, she didn't. Not one. "Well, good luck with that."

He caught her hand, threaded his fingers through hers. "I was hoping you'd come with me."

Torn between the desire to spend time with him and the knowledge it just wasn't smart, she drew in a breath, let it out slowly. "Do you think that's a good idea?"

"Probably not," he answered honestly. "Come anyway."

"You make it hard to say no."

"Then don't."

"Jason."

"Come on, Cherry, it's only a couple of hours. And we'll be in public surrounded by people. Nothing can happen." All good arguments. Then he hit her with the sucker punch. "It's for Rikki."

"Okay," she pulled at her captive hand, "but you have to keep your hands to yourself." She hated to make the condition, but knew it was the only way she'd make it through the afternoon with her sanity intact.

He kissed her hand before releasing her. "If you insist."

The seductive warmth of his breath on her skin almost changed her mind, but she held strong. "Let me secure the tent, and I'll be ready to go."

"Great." To his credit, he didn't gloat. "How can I help?"

Cherry told him and they were soon climbing into his truck headed for the local supermart. He practically crowed when she clued him into the fact the shoes were in the toy department.

Inside the store, he manhandled a cart free, then led the way to the toys. He obviously knew his way around that department, which made her truly wonder at a man's ability to achieve tunnel vision when it came to the girly things in life. Especially when he had a daughter turning three. Cherry had wondered if he'd used the whole princess shoes ploy to steal some time alone with her, but the look of bafflement on his face as he faced the assortment of gilt and fluffy shoes disabused her of that notion. The man was truly at a loss here.

Taking pity on him, she snagged a gold pair, topped by the softest of white feathers threaded through with more gold. She'd have died for a pair like them when she was a kid.

Tossing them into his cart, she assured him, "Guaranteed gaudy enough to make Rikki squeal."

He sighed his relief. "Thanks."

She just grinned and selected a matching tiara that she placed in the basket. "What else is on your list?"

He recited a lengthy list that she ruthlessly cut in half. Rikki didn't need things to know she was loved. Cherry recognized some of the items he'd told her about the other day at the BeeHive, and they stuck with those, sans the pony and the little brother.

Then she found out he already had the pony hidden in the barn at home.

"Of course," she acknowledged as if it were expected. This was Texas, after all.

"I'm not sure she'll ever have a little brother. Even if I could control such things, I don't know. I really haven't thought about marrying again."

Hearing the pain in his voice, Cherry broke the no-touching rule to rub the back of his arm, wanting to soothe him. "You will when the time is right. Until then, there's no reason to rush it."

"I met Diane my sophomore year in college. She was a freshman. So fresh and sweet, I couldn't take my eyes off her. We clicked right from the beginning. Within six months, we had our lives mapped out." He blindly reached for a bag of beef jerky, threw it into the cart. "It didn't include Diane dying."

His sorrow and loneliness were so strong they breached the protective guards Cherry used to shield herself from sensory overload. She knew he'd be outraged if he thought she was reading him.

But she didn't need her special talents to see how he suffered. Or to recognize he rarely, if ever, spoke of his feelings.

"You can't lose the love you had with her. It'll always be a part of you. I've taken a lot of online courses on psychiatry and counseling. Many reports show surviving spouses of loving relationships remarry fairly soon. The conclusion is they're seeking that happy union again."

His blank expression effectively hid his reaction to her words. The fact he continued to listen spoke volumes. She decided to push her luck with one last piece of advice.

"You may never remarry, but if you do, you should look on it as a tribute to the happiness you shared. Not as a betrayal."

He didn't answer, but he nodded. She'd given him something to think about. She only hoped it helped him in the long run.

In the meantime, to distract him, she drew him toward the little girls' department, into the middle of frou-frou land. He dragged his feet, a sure sign her tactic was working.

"Hannah usually does this girly stuff," he complained.

"Buck up, it's almost over."

"You're enjoying this."

"Well, yeah. When's the party?"

He laughed. "You mean Rikki didn't tell you? It's Saturday afternoon."

Cherry rejoiced at the sound of his amusement. "Yes, I remember now." She held up two frilly dresses, one pink, one blue. "Which?"

"The pink," he said without hesitation. He took the hanger from her and held the dress aloft. All ruffles and lace, it embodied a little girl's dream. "She'll love this."

Cherry agreed.

He added it to the items in the cart and headed for the checkout. Soon they were on the way back to the fairgrounds.

Cherry hated to have their time together end. Realistically, she knew no future existed for them. That wouldn't stop her from stealing every moment with him she could. How many more opportunities she'd get, she didn't know.

Several townspeople had stopped Jason to say hello and to ogle her. Everyone had been friendly, but she'd received a few disapproving glances. Remembering those gazes, she suggested Jason drop her at the edge of the fairgrounds so they didn't have to go past the picketers that had taken up residence at the front gate.

He insisted on seeing her all the way to her tent. As she approached the tent, she felt something was off. Someone had been inside; she knew it before she released the locks holding the front flaps together.

Inside, the furniture had been upended, posters torn in pieces, the scarves pulled down and stomped on. A sticky pink mess covered everything. One whiff and Cherry knew.

"Cotton candy," she whispered, appalled by the destruction. She bent and picked up one of Nona's favorite scarves. "Who would do this?"

Jason had the grim suspicion he knew. Maybe not the actual perpetrators, but the committee responsible. Moving to the back of the tent, he examined the three-foot high slash in the back panel. A good-sized knife would be needed to penetrate the thick canvas.

"Is anything missing?" Beyond the vandalism against Cherry, he detested the thought of anyone being on the fairgrounds with a weapon, let alone a knife big enough to do this job.

She looked around with sorrowful eyes. "No." Tears running down her cheeks, Cherry righted the table.

"Leave it." Jason went to her, took her hands in his. "I'm calling Sheriff McCabe. You need to report this."

"What good will it do?" she demanded, and he saw the effort it cost her to keep her voice steady. "The damage is already done. I just want to clean up the mess and put it behind me."

"I know." He wrapped her in his arms. It hurt to see her distress. "Do it for me. I want a record of this. I'm not going to let this go unanswered."

She laid her head on his chest. "Just let it go."

Her woeful plea only made him more determined. "It's important to me."

With a sigh, she nodded.

Pulling his cell out, he dialed Trace, explained the situation and asked him to come. Then Jason just held her.

"I'm used to suspicion," she spoke to his chest, head bowed, "to the distrust that always comes with being a stranger, but we've never been targeted like this. We've never had our things destroyed, our space vandalized." She rubbed at her cheeks. "I don't like it."

He didn't like it, either. Didn't like seeing this proud, feisty, giving woman brought low by a mean-spirited action of devastation and cowardice.

He'd tried to put her kisses out of his mind. To put

her out of his mind. He had no business thinking about her, wanting her, touching her. His business was his daughter and the city of Blossom.

"The Strong family helped settle Blossom over a hundred years ago," he said, wanting to distract her, needing to distract himself. "They started the Strong Bank and Trust and began building a community. Every generation, a Strong has taken on the responsibility of leading the town. Blossom prospered and in 1889 was named the county seat. This is the first time I've ever been ashamed of my city."

"Don't." She lifted her head, palmed the tears from her eyes. "I'm the outsider here. Don't condemn the whole for the actions of a few."

He couldn't answer her. Instead, he led her outside to wait. A food booth nearby was open and he got her a cup of coffee, added a bunch of sugar and sat her down to wait. Trace arrived ten minutes later.

He began his investigation and Cherry paced. As the shock wore off and her dander rose, she became more and more antsy.

Trace inspected the damage, snapped a few pictures and took Cherry's and Jason's statements.

"We'll check around, see if anyone saw anything. We dusted the posters and furniture for prints, beyond that there's not much we can do." He spoke compassionately, but Cherry wanted the facts. She wanted action.

Trace shrugged. "I'll let you know as soon as I have something. You're free to reenter the tent. I can give you the name of some cleaning companies in town if you'd like."

Her expression tight, Cherry shook her head. "No, I'll do it. Thanks for your help, you've been very kind."

He tipped his hat at her. "All part of the service." He caught Jason's eye. "Can I have a word with you?"

Jason had kept close to Cherry, lending his support, adding his impressions. Her simmering anger rattled him. He didn't want her to face the cleanup on her own:

"Wait for me," he urged her. "I'll help you."

"That's not necessary," she protested tightly, turning on her heel.

He caught her arm. "It is to me."

Her eyes flashed, but she didn't argue further. "Suit yourself." Pulling free, she headed for her tent.

Jason turned his attention to Trace, who was watching Cherry's retreat. He inclined his head in her direction. "What's going on with you and the fortune-teller?"

Jason crossed his arms over his chest. "Unfortunately, nothing."

"Doesn't look like nothing."

He frowned his displeasure. "What? Did my mom leave you in charge when she left for Europe?"

"Come on, Jason, I'm thinking of you. And of Cherry. You've seen the picketers out front. Half the signs are aimed at the fortune-teller. Seeing you spending time with her will only aggravate the protesters."

"I'm not living my life to the dictates of protesters."

"Don't be an ass. This isn't just about you, or Cherry, either. This is about stirring up trouble between the townspeople and the carnies, the pro-carnival and the CMB supporters, the locals and the out-of-towners. I need you working with me, not against me."

"Which is exactly why there's nothing going on between Cherry and me. That doesn't mean I'm going to leave her to the mercies of the CMB and their protesters, especially when they're carrying large knives."

Trace shoved back his hat. "Jason, you can't think Bitsy Dupres would sanction the use of weapons. This is the work of punks using the dispute to cause trouble."

"Fine." Jason respected Trace enough to let him do his job. But he also had the safety of his townspeople and the fairgoers to consider. "Prove it. In the meantime, I want two deputies posted at the front gate. We can't search everyone, but I want everyone to know we're on alert."

Trace gave him their index finger salute, acknowledging agreement but letting Jason know he owed Trace for the extra service. "You got it, but remember what I said." He gestured toward Cherry. "For her sake."

Jason frowned, but nodded. Then he remembered something else he'd been meaning to talk to Trace about. "The other day, Cassie was going on about the Swindle and included Bitsy's name in a list of victims."

Trace's eyebrows lifted. "Bitsy wasn't a victim of the Swindle."

"That's what I said. She quickly corrected herself, but I want you to check it out. Something's off here. I've always thought there was an informer who provided information for the con."

"Yeah, lucky how they targeted families with enough money to invest." Trace made a note. "I'll check it out."

"Be discreet," Jason said. "I don't want the informer alerted or Bitsy embarrassed."

Trace tucked his notebook in his pocket. "I'll handle it personally."

He took off. A moment later, Jason ducked into the tent to help Cherry. She shot him a quick unreadable glance before turning back to the cleanup. They worked in silence for the most part and shortly had the debris cleared out. She scrubbed on the cotton candy while Jason located some gray tape to seal up the slash in the back.

He stood back to examine his handiwork. "That should hold until I get someone out here to stitch it up."

She joined him, eyeing the repair job with a jaundiced gaze, but all she said was, "Thank you. I have a friend in the troupe who handles canvas repairs."

"Of course." He'd forgotten she had a support group of her own. Which was good. She wasn't alone. Yet somehow he wasn't relieved.

No, he hadn't been able to get her or the kiss they'd shared out of his mind. Not since his wife died had he been so enthralled with a woman. Felt so alive. He knew better, yet he'd still found himself seeking her out.

He grabbed her hand. "I'm sorry this happened."

Her dark eyes lifted to his. He saw a mix of emotions in the chocolate depths: regret, sadness, resignation and more.

"So am I." She gently freed her hand from his grasp. "I don't blame you. But this does reinforce our decision to stick to our own worlds. Today was nice, but it can't happen again."

As she thanked him for his help and walked away, he realized they were further apart now than when he'd arrived at her tent this morning.

Extra props were stored in the unit under the trailer. Cherry recruited Carlo to help her cart the replacement furniture over to the tent.

Once everything was in place, he inspected the repair job on the back slit. "Jordan does good work. Damn crazies, bringing knives to the fair. Why can't people just have fun?"

"Some people don't know how. Especially if they're feeling threatened."

"You're too soft, Cherry. These people attacked you. You must be on guard at all times. I've got the troupe on alert. Your tent and trailer will be watched."

"Thanks, Carlo. I don't know what I'd do without you." And she didn't. The troupe's "prince," Carlo was a rock. Because of him, the troupe had the best safety rating of any carnival in the country. Because of him, the troupe got their choice of fairs. Because of him, Cherry was in Blossom City.

"I don't like you being alone. Since Rose is not here, perhaps you should have one of the dancers stay with you."

"If I get spooked, I'll ask someone, but really I prefer my privacy." She threaded the sheer gold panels on to the rod; both had survived the rampage on the tent intact. He went to the other end and in a moment they had the rod in place.

"The sheriff is looking into the incident. It would please me if you encouraged the troupe to cooperate."

He stared at her from silvery eyes. He wore his black-brown hair swept back in a ponytail, and with his Latin good looks, he caused a stir among the local girls everywhere the troupe went. His scar only added to his bad-boy allure. Too bad there'd never been any passion between them. No. That would be too convenient, too easy.

Rumor was he'd spent time behind bars. She found it hard to believe. He had more integrity than anyone she'd ever met. She did know he preferred to keep troupe business within the troupe. And when it came to dealing with public officials, he let Flannery, the troupe's manager, handle things.

Flannery wasn't exactly Cherry's favorite person right now. He'd been the one to negotiate the deal with Blossom County that left her out in the cold.

Carlo looked none too pleased with her request to be left alone, but eventually he nodded. "This town has problems of its own. The sheriff will probably be too busy with that to follow up with our business. But

I don't like the use of the knife, the destruction of property. We'll make his investigation easy from this side. I'll pass the word."

"You're my hero." She lifted onto tiptoes, kissed his cheek. "Things should get better tomorrow when the fair opens."

"Better would be you staying out of trouble. Better yet would be you staying away from the mayor."

It didn't surprise Cherry that Carlo knew about her and Jason—what there was to know. She may be psychic, but Carlo had sources.

"You get your wish. The plan is he's staying in his world and I'm staying in mine."

"Sounds like a good plan." He held a poster so she could affix Velcro patches to the back, then pressed it into place on the tent wall. "It's not smart to have a cotton candy fling with a public figure."

"Yeah." She glanced around the tent she'd scrubbed earlier, that still smelled of cotton candy and soap. "I've had all the cotton candy I can handle."

Chapter Eight

Tuesday, the first day of the fair dawned bright and hot. Not one cloud marred the vivid blue of the vast sky. Cinnamon and coffee spiced the air, ready to tempt early fair goers when the gates opened.

Cherry crunched on raisin bran out of a plastic cup on her way to her tent. The gates would open in fifteen minutes. Most fairs chose to open soft, on a midweek day, so glitches could be found and fixed before the crowds descended on the weekends. Some acts, like the belly dancers, waited to open in the afternoon and went late.

When Nona worked with Cherry, they'd split, one taking the early hours and the other taking the late hours. Working on her own, she planned to work early and close about eight. She'd flex the hours if necessary, but traditionally the crowds swarmed for the rides and games during the late hours.

Besides readings, she sold a few mystic items— crystals, fairy dust and tarot cards. Luckily, she hadn't moved her inventory in before the tent was vandalized. She also taught tarot reading. The classes were amazingly popular.

"Hey, Cherry." Hudson, a rouster on Carlo's crew stepped into the tent.

"Morning, Hudson." Cherry finished arranging her display and gave the short, muscular man her attention. "What can I do for you?"

Hudson removed his cowboy hat revealing a buzz cut. He turned the hat repeatedly in strong, squat fingers. A cocky, confident man, his nervousness was jarringly out of character.

"I was wondering if you could help me."

"Sure, what's up?" She waved him toward a chair, but he shook off the offer.

"There's this woman, a local lady, brown hair to here," he indicated the top of his shoulder. "Always looks stern. Do you know who I mean?"

The description didn't ring any bells. Cherry shook her head. "I'm sorry, I don't know who you're talking about."

"I know her from somewhere. Something's not good about this woman. I was hoping you could help me remember where I saw her."

"I'm willing to give it a try. What do you mean by something's not good about her?"

He shrugged powerful shoulders. "Something seems off, I don't know, out of place."

"Well, let's give it a try. What I need is for you to visualize her while I concentrate." Because he chose to stand, Cherry did as well. She bowed her head and closed her eyes.

She tried to blank her mind, but a sense of anxiety, of nervousness and despair, flooded her thoughts. The emotions were distinctly female, but not connected with Hudson.

Someone close by intruded on the reading.

Cherry opened her eyes and sought the source. The front flaps were pulled back, but nobody within view seemed to be paying attention to them.

Noticing her distraction, Hudson asked, "Is something wrong?"

"I'm sorry, Hudson. I'm picking up something. A woman in distress, but it's not your lady."

"Do not worry." He pulled on his hat. "I will check with you later."

He stepped outside and disappeared. Immediately, a head popped around from the right front flap. A head topped by stringy blond hair pulled back in a clip. Melissa rounded the corner and came fully into view. She wore the same oversized clothes as when Cherry had met her nearly a week ago, the same lost expression.

"Hello, Melissa."

"Lady Pandora. I brought money for a reading."

Her desperate eagerness preceded her into the tent. "I can pay you."

"Melissa." Cherry escorted her to a chair, then sat down across from her. Someone needed to help this child-woman. Cherry longed to be that person, but refused to risk hurting the girl more than helping her. "I can't take your money. I need your parents' permission to read for you."

Melissa's face fell, her shoulders slumped, her eyes pleaded. "Can't you just tell me if he's coming back?"

"Why don't you tell me who he is?" Cherry knew she should resist the urge to interfere, but she couldn't let the girl run off again without at least trying to convince her to see a doctor.

She expected Melissa to perk up. *He* was obviously her savior and Cherry had just given her the opportunity to talk him up.

Instead, Melissa stared longingly at the tarot cards stacked on the table. "Aren't you going to use the cards?"

"I'm not doing a reading. We're just going to talk for a while. Tell me about your boyfriend."

"He's not my boyfriend," she mumbled. Frowning, she toyed with the fringe on the velvet scarf covering the table. "I mean he was, until my dad spoiled everything."

"How did he spoil things?"

"He came and took me home."

"Why?"

She sneered. "Because he loves me."

"You don't think your father loves you?"

Melissa looked up and blinked. She appeared shocked by the question. "Of course he loves me." Her chin dropped lower. "But he doesn't trust me." She knuckled away a tear. "I disappoint him."

"If he loves you, he can learn to trust again. But not if you continue to hide from him."

"You don't know." She stopped playing with the fringe to bury her hands in her lap and her shoulders stooped forward even more to protect her body. "You don't understand."

"I don't need the details to understand human nature." Cherry fought the urge to comfort, to touch. "It's instinctive to distrust people when we know they're not being honest with us, especially people we love. Because it hurts that much more."

Melissa shook her head, and closed in on herself even more. "You don't know."

Cherry sighed and made one last attempt to get through to her. "Melissa, look at me. Listen to me." Slowly the girl lifted her head. "I do know."

Melissa's eyes grew wide.

"I also know you've made yourself miserable and you're hurting more than yourself. Do you understand me?" Cherry waited until Melissa nodded. "You're not a child any longer, you have responsibilities."

She sat up straighter and nodded again.

"You're tired and hungry and dirty. Go home, eat something healthy, and take a shower. Once you feel better, you need to rethink what you're doing and take some responsible action. And you need to trust in your father's love."

Worrying her lip, Melissa stood. "I don't know if he'll listen. He's already so disappointed."

Cherry walked with her to the front of the tent. "Then what do you have to lose?"

"Everything," Melissa whispered, her eyes stark pools of fear. She pulled her oversized shirt closed over her oversized form and turned to leave. "Thank you for talking with me."

Sensing she'd made some headway into the girl's uncertainty, Cherry decided to give one more push. "Melissa," she called and, gaining the teenager's attention, quietly revealed, "He's not coming back."

Cherry sighed when Melissa simply turned and walked away. She hoped with all her soul she'd gotten through to the girl.

"Cherry! Cherry!" An excited voice trilled. Cherry swung around in time to catch Rikki Strong as she launched her small body at Cherry.

"Hey, squirt." Cherry looked over the little girl's head to her father who was a few steps behind her.

He had his gaze on the retreating Melissa. When he reached Cherry's side, he issued a warning. "Be careful in any dealings with Melissa Tolliver. There's trouble there."

"What do you mean? Do you know Melissa?"

"I know her father better. Rev. Tolliver is a stalwart supporter of the CMB. He's been one of the outspoken protesters against the carnival."

Cherry had a bad feeling about that news. "Does his reason have anything to do with Melissa?"

"Everything. Seven or eight months ago, the superstore hired a carnival group to set up on their property. Melissa hooked up with one of the carnies and when they left town, she went with them."

"She ran away?"

Jason nodded. "It took Rev. Tolliver a month to locate her and bring her home. She's kept to herself ever since."

His revelation pretty much confirmed Cherry's suspicions of what happened. Except she hadn't anticipated the complication of Rev. Tolliver or his involvement with the CMB. Thankfully she hadn't actually given the girl a reading.

"Thanks for the warning." She flipped Rikki's ponytail around a finger. "What are you guys doing here?"

Rikki jumped up and down. "Daddy bringed me to the fair for my birthday. We came to say hello."

"Well, it's my lucky day." Cherry hugged the three-year-old and met Jason's gaze over her head. She slanted an eyebrow at him. "You keep breaking the rules."

"What rules?" he asked all innocence. "I just came by to make sure you were all right after yesterday's ransacking."

"Almost as good as new." She tried to make light of the distressing incident. "I talked to Carlo and he's going to ensure the carnies cooperate with the sheriff."

"Good to know. I checked with Trace before coming over here. He didn't have anything new to report."

"Cherry." Rikki tugged on Cherry's hand, demanding her attention. "Can you go with us?"

Cherry considered. Without doubt, her answer should be no. She'd already tempted fate this morning by talking with Melissa Tolliver. But she wanted to go, to spend time with Jason, with his precocious daughter. Yesterday had been such a trial; she longed to steal today for herself.

She thought of the tiara gift wrapped in her trailer and made her decision.

Deliberately keeping her attention on Rikki, she said, "Oh, I think I can take a couple of hours to spend with a special birthday girl."

"Goody." Rikki clapped her hands. "Daddy, Cherry's going to see the fair with us."

"I heard." He met Cherry's gaze. "Are you sure you can take the time?"

"Mornings are slow," she justified to herself as well as to him. Then she flat-out confessed, "And I want to show you my fair."

His eyes warmed as he reached out to tuck a stray corkscrew curl behind her ear. "Then lock up and let's go."

It took only a few minutes to do just that, then they were off. Cherry clasped Rikki's hand and made a point of placing the girl between the adults. Cherry led them down the midway, introducing them to friends.

Rikki, with her big blue-gray eyes, curly brown ponytail and instant-friendship attitude, paved the way for acceptance of Jason. The energetic little girl won hearts wherever they went. By the time Cherry introduced him as the mayor, Rikki had softened them up with her bright smile and insatiable curiosity.

The fact he was with Cherry also scored him some points.

Carnies were nothing if not loyal.

Cherry took them first to the kiddie rides where they met up with Carlo. Cherry ignored the two men sizing each other up to point out a child-sized roller coaster to Rikki.

Her eyes popped wide and she jumped up and down. "Will you come with me, Cherry?"

"Sure." Cherry agreed. The miniature version was just her speed.

"Where do we get tickets?" Jason pulled out his wallet.

Carlo waved him off. "You're friends of Cherry. And it's the little one's birthday. Today you are our guests."

Jason demurred but Carlo insisted, as Cherry knew he would. Their male posturing amazed her, especially as there was no prize to be had. Certainly not her. Carlo was the closest she'd ever come to having a brother, and Jason the love she'd never have in her life.

Whatever they had to hash out, she was leaving them to it.

"Come on, Rikki, let's go." Clasping Rikki's hand, Cherry led the excited child toward the roller coaster.

"What about Daddy?" she demanded.

"He's too big." Cherry explained as they were buckled in. "Hold on tight."

Grinning ear to ear, Rikki wrapped her tiny fingers around the bar and shrieked when the ride started. Cherry's ears rang by the time they stopped.

Once off the ride, Rikki ran to Jason and told him all about it. As if he hadn't watched every moment and waved every time she went roaring by.

Carlo was nowhere to be seen. Jason revealed the other man had been called away.

"Look! Look at the boats." Rikki pointed. "I want to go there."

She started to run, but Jason snagged her hand. "Slow down."

"Daddy," she wailed. Tipping her head back, she looked way, way up to see his face. Whatever she saw there made her slow down. But didn't worry her too much. She swung his hand back and forth, then reached for Cherry's hand, too. "Hurry."

Cherry met Jason's gaze and at the same moment they lifted Rikki off her feet and ran to the next ride, little boats that went round and round. She shrieked with glee.

No hope of Cherry fitting in those seats, which put her on the sidelines. With Jason.

"She's having a great time." He threaded his fingers through hers on the plastic railing. "Thank you."

Skin touched skin and feelings got mixed up with emotions that got mixed up with physical reaction. First, the heat struck her and the want to reciprocate, followed by the instinctive urge to pull back in self-preservation, side by side with the rush of sheer joy and restrained desire from him.

Too much to absorb and analyze in mere seconds. She focused on the positive uncomplicated joy she felt coming from him. Simple joy in the day, in spending time with his daughter, in being with Cherry.

How could she resist the lure of pure happiness?

Especially when she perceived how rarely Jason gave in to such moments. What harm was there in taking a few hours of happiness, in living for the present? She already knew it was going to hurt when it came time to leave. Why not enjoy what fate handed her?

"You don't have to thank me. I'm having fun, too."

"Come on." He nudged her shoulder with his. "You're at the fair all the time. This must be old hat for you."

She squeezed his fingers, holding on tight to him, to the moment. "It's times like this that make every day new. I should thank you. The fair is magic, but every once in a while we need a reminder. Nothing like the delight of a child to do that."

Rikki proved that as she raced toward them. She chattered all the way to the next ride, little cars that went round and round.

And so it went, Rikki enjoying the rides, Cherry and Jason enjoying each other.

After the rides, they moved on to games. Cherry winked at Sam in the Toss and Pitch; his slip of the foot resulted in a stuffed elephant for Rikki's efforts. At the food booth, Rikki wanted cotton candy, but Cherry talked her into caramel apple slices. She couldn't stomach the smell of the candy concoction after cleaning it off her canvas walls.

Eventually, they wound up back at Cherry's tent.

When they stopped by the twins' tent earlier for a private lesson in belly dancing for Rikki, Cherry recruited the twins' help in retrieving her gift from her trailer and bringing it to her tent. The twins kept backup keys for her, and she kept a set for them.

The gaily wrapped package was waiting when she unlocked the padlocks on the zippers and let Jason and Rikki into the tent. Jason went to check out the repair job on the back panel.

"I have something for you Rikki." Cherry picked up the present. "Happy birthday."

Rikki's eyes lit up. "For me?"

"Just for you. With special princess wrapping paper."

Rikki leaned forward to look. "Pretty."

"It's okay, go ahead." Cherry offered the package. "Open it."

"But it's not my party." Rikki protested, placing her hands behind her back. "I'm not supposed to open my presents until my party. Daddy said so."

"Sweetheart, I won't be at your party. I'm sure it'll be okay if you open this present today."

"Uh-huh," Rikki said. "I want you to come to my party. It's on Saturday."

Cherry deliberately didn't look at Jason. "Oh, I don't think that's a good idea."

"Why?" the little girl wanted to know.

"Well, I have to work."

"Can't you get the day off? Daddy's taking the day off."

"Yeah, can't you take the day off?" Jason spoke up tempting her and encouraging his daughter.

Cherry turned to him, sending him a telling look. She lowered her voice. "I'm thinking of you here. You know it's not a good idea."

"It's Rikki's birthday party, and she wants you there." His eyes said he wanted her there, too.

It was a mistake, common sense told her that. But why start listening to common sense now? God help her, she wanted to go.

"Okay. I'll be there."

Chapter Nine

Cherry turned right onto Strong Road, the private drive that led to the Strong home. She expected the house to quickly come into view, but the road wound on and on. A herd of cattle roamed a rock-and-brush-strewn pasture to the left. To the right, more of the same terrain gave way to a lake in the distance.

A good mile or more off the main road, the house loomed large on the horizon. House? Try manor, complete with columns and a veranda that circled what she could see of the two-story building. Several out buildings, including a large barn with attached corrals housing a number of horses, confirmed this was a working ranch. The sprawling old oak trees littered throughout the compound told the story of how long the Strongs had occupied this land.

So not only did the Strongs own the Strong Bank and Trust on the square, but they owned a working ranch as well.

From what she'd heard, their family had been one of the founding families of Blossom. What must it be like to have roots like that? To trace your family back and find them in history books as mayors, governors, congressmen. She'd run the Strong name on the Internet, found Jason was the latest in a long line of politicians. That this house had been the home of seven generations of Strongs.

For a woman who'd never known a home without four wheels, who'd never known her father's name, let alone how many generations his people had been wherever, the cultural differences were more than a little sobering.

Parking her truck alongside Hannah's Lexus brought back a painful memory. Because they were on the road so much, Nona had home schooled Blossom. When she was eleven, Blossom begged to be allowed to go to regular school over the winter season while they were "resting over" in Florida. Nona gave in, but Blossom hated the experience. In many ways she was more advanced than the other children, but in other ways she was far behind and she didn't do well in tests.

She'd been miserable. The regular kids didn't like her because she was new, and strange, and it was the middle of the semester and they already had their friends. Her carny friends wouldn't talk to her because they felt she thought she was better than them by wanting to go to the regular school.

When spring came and the carnival moved on, Cherry had been glad to leave the school behind. She never forgot the experience and to this day had a phobia about taking tests in the real world.

It's why she didn't have her GED. Why she hadn't pursued a career as a midwife.

Grabbing the princess wrapped package off the front seat, locking up her truck, and walking past the Lexus, a Mercedes and an Excursion made her feel as if she were being tested all over again. It took all her backbone not to turn around and drive away.

The warmth in Jason's eyes when he opened the door made her glad she'd stuck it out.

"Hello, beautiful." He took her hand and drew her inside, lifting her arm and sending her into a twirl that fluttered the handkerchief hem of her pink-and-purple sundress. "You look lovely."

She took in his white dress shirt, black jeans and black bolo tie. "You look pretty yummy yourself."

He led her through a living room outfitted in brown suede furnishings and cream carpeting to the back veranda. She set her gift on a credenza already stacked high with gifts before stepping outside where several adult couples sat in the shade, watching children play on a wide patch of grass.

A rose garden complete with gazebo bordered the lawn to the right and disappeared around the side of the house. A fenced pool area was off to the left.

"Rikki," Jason called. "Come say hello to Cherry."

"Cherry." Rikki came running followed by a passel of other kids. She wrapped her little arms around Cherry's knees. "You came. Yeah."

"Wouldn't miss it," Cherry assured her, glad she hadn't chickened out.

"These are my friends." Rikki rattled off a list of names Cherry had no hope of following. Not a problem since the kids immediately scrambled back to their game of tag.

"Hannah's over here." Jason's hand in the small of her back directed her toward the adults seated in patio furniture.

To Cherry's relief she recognized several faces—the sheriff, Cindy Tucker and Blake Gray Feather. And seated on a bench out on the lawn watching over the kids were Dutch and Buster, flirting with Mrs. Davis and Mrs. White.

"Everyone, this is Cherry Cooper." Jason made a sweeping introduction. The doorbell rang inside. "I've got to get that. Hannah, make sure she meets everyone."

Hannah did her duty as asked, introducing her husband, Daniel, then the rest of the friends and neighbors gathered around. She surprised Cherry by rising and coming around to give her a hug.

"I'm so glad you came." She pulled Cherry a little ways down the veranda. "Rikki's talked of nothing but you, and her day at the fair."

"We all had fun," Cherry said.

"I know, which is pretty amazing for Jason. Diane died so soon after Rikki's birth he associates one with the other. He puts on a good face, but it's a hard time for him. You made it easier this year. Thank you."

"Well." Cherry had no words. "I'm glad."

"Me, too. And that's not all." Hannah clasped Cherry's hands and her face lit up like a Christmas tree. "Later, I'm going to be making an announcement of my own."

"Oh, Hannah, congratulations." Cherry felt the peace and joy in the other woman. "I'm so happy for you."

"You've been good for all of us, Cherry. Especially Jason. I haven't seen him so alive in years. He cares about you."

"Hannah, you're wrong. There's nothing serious going on between Jason and me."

"Just don't hurt him," Hannah pleaded. "He's more vulnerable than he appears. Control is so important to him he comes across as invincible."

"Yeah, I've noticed his need to keep everything just so."

"He's always been strong, a leader, but the need for control got worse after he lost Diane. He was the same way after Dad died. He even tried to keep me from going away to college." Hannah bit her lip, obviously uncertain about revealing family secrets. She searched Cherry's features, her eyes and must have found reassurance because she continued. "It's as if by maintaining control, by keeping everything the same most of the time, he can prevent us from being hurt."

"So he doesn't lose anyone else."

"In a nutshell."

"Well, we all handle grief in our own way."

"I'm glad you understand. You're just what Jason needs. I'm so glad he met you." Hannah didn't wait for a response but pulled Cherry back into the fold of partygoers.

Under Hannah's warm example, everyone quickly absorbed Cherry into their midst. The initial reservations, hers and the other guests', faded as regular conversation and witty exchanges remained impersonal.

Jason reappeared. "Strange. That was Cassie, Frank and the kids but they dropped off their gift and left."

"That is weird," Hannah agreed. "I spoke to Cassie earlier and she said they were planning to come. How odd to get here, then leave. Of course, she's been acting strange all week."

"Their loss." He rubbed his hands together. "I've got great steaks to put on the grill."

"Sounds good. When do we eat?"

"Potatoes are baking in the oven. You throw together a salad, and I'll fire up the grill."

"Deal. I'm starved. Cherry, can you carry the steaks out to the grill?"

"Sure, lead me to them." The kitchen was a cook's dream—chrome, white and slate-gray, two ovens, an island workspace and a subzero freezer refrigerator. "Wow."

"Fabulous, isn't it. My mom's haven. She's in Europe with my aunt for a month. London, Paris, Madrid. I'm so jealous."

Cherry peeked into a pantry, found shelves stocked better than some stores she'd shopped. "Of the kitchen or the trip?"

Hannah laughed. "Both, truth be told." She pulled a large pan from the refrigerator. "Here are the steaks."

"Hello, Hannah. We let ourselves in." An older woman in cream linen slacks and cotton twin set entered the kitchen, followed by a younger woman in a lightweight skirt and capped-sleeved tee. Both women were blond and shared a strong family resemblance. "I brought a macaroni salad."

Bitsy Dupres, unofficial leader of the CMB. They'd met once when Bitsy approached Cherry and appealed to her sense of common decency to leave Blossom County. As if her mere presence threatened the moral judgment of the city's youth.

"Great, we're just getting ready to start the steaks." Hannah accepted the large bowl, slid it into the fridge. "Bitsy, Elizabeth Dupres, this is Cherry Cooper."

Elizabeth smiled and offered her hand. "Hello, you're the fortune-teller from the fair. Tammy Wright is a friend of mine. She's absolutely thrilled with her little girl."

Cherry forced a smile. "She did the hard part, I just made a prediction." She nodded at the older woman who kept her hands to herself. "Mrs. Dupres."

"Miss Cooper." Bitsy acknowledged, then turned to Jason's sister. "Hannah, is Jason around?"

"Out by the barbecue. If you're going that way, can you take this pan of steaks out to him?"

"Certainly." Hefting the pan, she exited the kitchen, her low-heeled sandals clicking on the slate tiles.

Elizabeth's cheeks turned pink in embarrassment, her discomfort obvious.

"That leaves us on salad detail," Cherry quickly jumped into the silence, wanting to get past the awkward moment. "I'm pretty handy with a knife if you need chopping done."

"I'm sure we do." Hannah turned back to the refrigerator, keeping her tone cheerful. "We have tomatoes, onions, cucumbers. Oh, and Jason's barbecue sauce."

"I'll take it," Cherry volunteered, hoping to escape the kitchen for a few moments. She grabbed the bowl from Hannah's hand and a basting brush from a utensil caddy on the island, and dodged out the closest door. She ended up in uncharted territory. Sounds of the party came from the right and she saw the edge of the pool.

She neared the corner and heard Bitsy's too reasonable tones. Cherry hesitated, realizing the woman had lingered to talk to Jason after delivering the steaks.

"—thinking of you. Your political impartiality is

admirable. However, this is your home, and Rikki is an impressionable child."

"Rikki's the one who invited Cherry. It's her party." The effort for patience sounded in Jason's voice. But his answer made Cherry wonder if she'd misread his expression yesterday. Had she seen what she wanted to see? Was she here under sufferance?

"Of course she's enthralled by the flamboyance of the woman. You're the parent, it's up to you to protect her from the unsavory elements in life." Gentle reprimand dripped from each word.

"Bitsy, I understand your concern—"

He understood? Cherry held her breath, waiting to hear the word *but*. Waiting to hear Jason defend her, to hear him refute the unsavory comment.

"Thank you."

Thank you? Her breath escaped on a sob she cut off with a hand over her mouth. Thank you?

Heartache deafened her to anything else he said. She swung on her heel and fled in full retreat. No need to listen any further. The barbecue sauce ended up on a side table outside the kitchen as she made her way around to the front of the house.

Thank God she had her keys in her pocket and she'd left her wallet in the truck.

How could she be so wrong about Jason?

So they had chemistry and had spent a few carefree moments together. So she made him hard, and he made her heart stutter. So they'd shared a few secrets and made each other laugh. So-what?

Nothing, that's what. Foolish of her to believe she was more important than his need to keep the peace.

Jason listened to his neighbor question his parenting skills and red rose to cloud his vision. He muttered something innocuous while counting to ten mentally. He needed to calm down before he told Bitsy Dupres exactly where to take her I-know-what's-best-for-you attitude.

"Thank you," he said. Yeah, thanks for nothing.

He gritted his teeth and counted to ten again, reminding himself she was a friend of his mother, a widow finding her place after the death of her husband. Reminding himself of the children playing nearby, of the audience farther down the porch, of the fact he was mayor and responsible for maintaining the peace.

Unsavory element. Unsavory element. Unsavory element. The words beat like a skipping CD in his mind. The idea of brave, sensitive, intelligent Cherry being dismissed in such narrow-minded terms ratcheted his blood pressure right back up.

He flipped the steaks, his fingers biting into the handle of the flipper. He continued to count. When he reached a hundred, he pinned Bitsy with a look that had her taking a step back.

"You're entitled to your opinion, Bitsy. You can picket the fair. You can sprout your righteous message to the masses. You can protest the unsightly appearance of two harmless old men on a public bench, and as mayor I'll defend your right to do so, for all the good any of it will do you." Temper ground his voice to fine gravel.

She blinked and pressed her lips tight. "I'm sure there's no need to take such a tone."

"Oh, there's a need. This is my home. Cherry Cooper is my guest. And nobody tells me what's best for my daughter."

Her blond, coiffed head went back, and she squared her shoulders defensively. "I only meant to help."

"No doubt."

"Perhaps I should leave." The words were half challenge, half plea.

"You're welcome to stay." He closed the lid to the barbecue, met her gaze straight on. "If you can control your urge to help me. And if you can treat my other guests with respect and courtesy."

He expected her to leave, on principle, and in a bit of a huff. But he underestimated her.

"For Rikki's sake." She nodded regally, pulled down the hem of her sweater and went to join the others around the patio table. Nobody seemed to have noticed the altercation between him and Bitsy.

Jason cooled his jets by walking across the yard to check on the kids.

"Daddy," Rikki came running over. "Is it time for cake?"

"No." He ran a teasing finger down her nose. "We have to eat dinner first. How do you want your steak?"

"There's only one way to eat a steak," she quoted.

"Rare," they said together.

"That's right." He slapped the little palm she held up for a high five. "Ten minutes more, then it's time to eat."

"Okay." She ran back to her friends.

Jason checked the steaks, then remembered the barbecue sauce. His boot heels rang against the wood porch on the way to the kitchen. He found the barbecue sauce on a table outside the kitchen door.

Hannah and Elizabeth looked up when he stepped inside.

"What's the barbecue sauce doing outside?" he asked. His gaze skidded around the room. "Where's Cherry?"

A frown touched Hannah's brow. "She took the barbecue sauce out to you."

"Damn." He stomped his way to the front, his thoughts replaying the scene with Bitsy. He had a bad feeling Cherry had heard enough to send her running.

Sure as aces over eights, her truck was gone and so was any chance of him enjoying the rest of the party. "Damn.

Jason threaded his way through trucks, trailers, and RVs. The carnival troupe campsite was pretty quiet, this being the time the midway ruled. Lights shone in several units, and a few people sat outside enjoying the cooler air, but he moved uncontested to Cherry's trailer.

She'd pointed it out the other day when she'd shown him her fair, and the world she lived in that was so different than the world where he abided. The carnival troupe, he'd learned, was a community in itself. There was a store, a school, an auto mechanic, even a clinic of sorts. In this world, people worked together, supported each other, protected one another.

After the festivities settled down at his place—which went on way longer than he'd had patience for—he'd sent Rikki home with Hannah. He'd cleaned up, showered and hopped in his truck, intent on finding Cherry and apologizing.

She hadn't been in her tent, so he hoped to find her here.

No time to lose. When he'd met Carlo the other day, along with assurances the carnies were assisting the sheriff in his inquiries, the man had warned Jason to be careful with Cherry, with her person and with her heart. Carlo made it very clear the entire troupe was watching over her, on the midway and in the caravan.

Any minute now, somebody'd be breathing down his neck. No doubt Carlo himself. Jason almost welcomed the chance to relieve a little tension with a knockdown, drag-out fight.

More important was speaking to Cherry, apologizing for being so damn slow to speak up. She probably wouldn't even believe he'd finally defended her.

Not that he had, really. Defended her. He'd been too busy keeping his cool, being the diplomat, defending his ground.

Lights shone from inside her trailer. He saw a dimming then release of light, movement. She was here.

He knocked. Waited. Knocked again.

"Cherry, it's Jason. I know you're in there."

The window in the door slid open. "Go away."

"I want to talk to you."

"We have nothing to talk about."

The light inside backlit her profile against the screen, reminding him of church and confessing his sins. The Good Lord forgave all. For all he felt like heaven in her arms, Cherry had more than a celestial body; she had heart and pride. And he'd injured both.

"You heard something at my house that upset you. I want to talk about that."

"Seems you had a chance to talk about that and chose not to."

"I know that's what you think."

"No." She sighed, a world of sadness in the sound. "It's what I heard."

Damn, the last thing he wanted was to hurt Cherry. The fact he cared more about protecting her feelings ahead of Bitsy's told him he'd fallen harder for the beautiful fortune-teller than was wise.

He couldn't let what they had end this way.

"Let me in. Let me see you. Let me explain."

"No need to explain. I understand only too well. You'll have to deal with Bitsy long after I've taken to the road again. Even when the sale goes through on the house for Nona and she settles here, our paths aren't likely to cross often. In fact, it should be easy to avoid each other. I suggest we start now."

"All of that's true, yes. Plus, Bitsy's a friend of my mother's. And she really does mean well. But none of that stopped me from nailing her hide to the wall."

"Really?" It was a wistful whisper.

"Yeah. My mom's going to rip into me when she gets home, but Bitsy questioning my parenting, denigrating you, that wasn't right. Not in my own home. Not when you were my guest."

"You're the mayor. You have to think beyond yourself."

"That's what I was telling myself while you were walking away. I'm sorry. Come out, let's talk."

The window closed. Her shadow moved away from the door.

Damn. He banged his head against the trailer, frustrated at his inability to convince her. Every day Rikki brought joy into his life, but he couldn't remember the last time he'd really laughed with a woman. His heart might feel that was a betrayal of Diane, but his mind and body really didn't want this to be the end.

The door rattled, opened, and Cherry stepped out, dressed all in leather. She handed him a helmet. "Let's take a ride."

His body snug against hers, they raced through the night, leaving the town and all it represented behind them. Jason reveled in the speed and the wind and the feel of her in his arms. If only they could go on forever. Leave their cares behind.

Finally, she turned back. He gave her directions and she rode nice and easy to a favorite spot of his overlooking the moonlit Strong Pond. She pulled to a stop under an old oak tree.

He led her over to a picnic table. They sat on the table, feet on the bench, facing the water.

"Great ride." He lifted her hand to his mouth, pressed a kiss to the center. "Thanks for coming out with me."

"I enjoyed it, too." She cupped his cheek in her hand, lowered his head to hers, and touched her lips to his. He needed no more prompting. Opening his mouth over hers, he drank her in. In moments, they were in each other's arms. Passion swept them up and away.

She fell back on the table, taking him with her. He unzipped her jacket, found lace and skin, dipped his head to sip and savor. Her fingers raked through his hair, held him to her as she arched under the twin assault of teeth and tongue.

She tugged at his shirt, dragged her nails down his back. He hummed his approval, worked his way up her throat, reclaimed her mouth in a slow slide into oblivion.

When her hands went for his zipper, he eased up, pulled back. Resting his forehead against hers, he sighed.

"We have to stop."

She groaned low in her throat. "Why?"

"Because I have no protection."

"Damn." She made that husky growl again and every nerve tingled down his spine.

"Yeah. Plus, if I pulled you out of this leather like I want to, you'd get splinters from this old table."

"Ouch. I imagine you'd prefer to stay splinter-free, as well. The grass?"

"Snakes. Plus there's that first thing I mentioned."

"A woman has the right to fantasize."

"Oh baby, you're a fantasy come true."

She trailed a finger up his side and back down again. "If you like me in my leather, you should see me in my tattoo."

His imagination went wild. He threw back his head and rolled to his back. "Sweet rose of Texas, I think I just swallowed my tongue."

A husky laugh added to his torment.

"You did that to torture me, right?"

"Frustration makes me mean."

"I think I like that about you."

Truth to tell, he liked a lot about her. Wishing for reassurances and absolutes, knowing both were impossible, he sat up, pulled her to sit in front of him. The moon, full and bright, was reflected in the still water of Strong Pond. The homestead was just over the rise to the right. He could trace his past back over a hundred years.

"This would be a lot easier if we knew what happens down the line." Though logic said there was no such thing as reading the future, she'd defied his beliefs more than once in the last couple of weeks. Jason asked, "What do you see for us?"

"It doesn't work that way," she explained. "I can't

read my own future. And you're a blank wall. I can pick up a few things from your past. Other than that, I have a hard time reading more than your mood."

He rested his chin on her shoulder. "You know that's kind of a relief."

She bumped her head against his. "Yeah, I figured."

"Answers would be nice, though." He tightened his arms around her.

"Life isn't that easy." She shared her dream of quitting the carnival and becoming a midwife. When he asked why she hadn't pursued her dream, she revealed her bad experience in Florida.

"You were a kid, Cherry. Give yourself a break. Heck, give the civilized world a break." He kissed her below her left ear. "You're brave and intelligent. And feisty as hell. You're capable of accomplishing anything you set your mind to doing."

"I'm not brave. I'm scared. Not just of the education thing."

"Of going on the road alone?"

"No, I can handle the road. Carlo, the twins, they'll help. Nona's the one who'll be alone. What if something happens to her? What if she's alone and has another fall? We've been together forever. She's over seventy. I don't want to lose these last years with her."

"Stay then." Jason couldn't believe the words coming out of his mouth. But they felt right. They felt real.

"Oh, that'll go over big with the CMB. Maybe I can set up shop right on the square."

"Well, maybe not on the square."

She laughed, equal parts humor and wistfulness. "I think I better stick with what I know."

Silence fell because, truth to tell, he couldn't in good faith as mayor encourage a fortune-teller to open up business in Blossom. No matter how much he wanted to jump her bones.

Chapter Ten

Not surprisingly, Cherry found sleep elusive. Around 5 a.m., she gave up trying. Coffee brewed while she showered and dressed. She poured the whole pot into a giant-sized thermos cup, grabbed the pictures she'd taken of the little yellow house and turned her truck toward Lubbock.

Nona greeted Cherry with open arms, hugging her close and holding on tight. "I've missed my girl."

"I've missed you more." Cherry stayed bent over the wheelchair while Nona rubbed her lipstick from Cherry's cheek. "How are you?"

"Better than ever. In a few minutes you can come with me to therapy, and I'll show you how well I walk. I practically don't need this chair any more." She patted the side of her wheelchair.

"That's great news. How much longer does the doctor say before you can leave here?"

"He says another two weeks, at least. Then I can leave anytime. I just need to have a place to go to. I'll have to continue therapy a couple of times a week for a month, but that's more to build up the strength in the leg."

"Great. I brought pictures of the yellow house I told you about."

She drew out the pictures and she and Nona pored over them. Nona loved the house on sight, just as Cherry knew she would.

"Lovely, just lovely." Nona patted the pictures together, set them aside. "Now tell me why you're really here."

"I just needed to see you. To remind myself who I am, and what my purpose in life is."

"I see. Questioning all things profound." She sat back and clasped her hands in her lap and considered Cherry. "Prince Charming got to you, didn't he?"

"I love him, Nona." It was a weight lifted just to confess the truth. To Nona and to herself. "I don't know what to do."

"Oh my child, you reach for it with both hands."

"I knew as soon as I touched him, just like you and Grandpa."

Nona reached for Cherry's hand. "You didn't tell me. I remember that moment with your grandpa. The attraction, the shock, the sheer overwhelming denial."

"Exactly. It was terrifying. And exhilarating. Nona, we're from two different worlds. Literally."

"So narrow it to one." Nona made it sound so simple.

"I can't. If I don't stay on the road, we won't be able to afford the house. You deserve to finally have a home of your own."

"You know better than that, Cherry. I've always had a home. Wherever you are is my home. Whatever makes you happy, makes me happy. And if you think I could be content tucked up in a house while you're miserable traveling the road, you're mistaken.

"You follow your heart, you hear me. I never regretted following your grandfather. Not for one day. We can rent instead of buying, build a Web site and advertise on the Internet, start an online business. Or you could take the tests you've been putting off, go for your midwife certification."

"Jason said I could do anything I set my mind to."

"Now see there, I like him already. 'Course, I've been telling you the same for years."

"So you have. When I'm with him, I feel prettier, smarter, braver. He makes me want to reach for the stars, makes me believe I can pluck them from the sky. And I fell for his three-year-old before I ever stopped being mad at him for keeping me from the fair."

Cherry sighed, pulled her legs up under her on the couch. "No need to change plans yet. Jason hasn't said how he feels. He may not be able to accept me into his world."

"You've explained how complex the dynamics are in town. But he's not the man you think he is if he lets you get away."

Tears welled up even as she grinned ear to ear. There, that's why she'd made the hundred-mile trip this morning. That unconditional love and support. Proof her thoughts were valid, not just wishful thinking.

"Never change, Nona." Cherry hugged her grandmother, holding her tight for a long moment. "I'm putting the papers in for the house. Even if things don't work out between Jason and me, you're still getting your home in Blossom."

Cherry drove back to Blossom City in much better spirits than when she'd left. Nona always helped her balance her thoughts. Being reminded of the big leap of faith Nona made to follow Grandpa into the carnival world and how she'd never regretted following her heart also helped.

Being psychic, Cherry, more than most, realized you made your choices and then you lived with them. If the choice didn't suit you, then you were faced with new choices.

But opportunities may never knock again.

She'd known attraction for Jason before she touched him and felt her world shift, fell in love with him despite that touch and the upheaval it promised in her life.

So maybe a relationship between them wasn't just a quirk of fate, but was meant to be.

As she flew down the dry and dusty Texas highway, she contemplated Jason's choices. Would he choose her in the face of the CMB's disapproval, with the Swindle still a recent memory?

She thought of the picketers at the fair gates and the vandalism of her tent and knew they'd face opposition if he did. Then she remembered the first time she came to Blossom City. She recalled the wounded spirit of the city and how she'd worried this might not be the best place for Nona to settle. But she'd changed her mind because she'd also felt the optimism of the future for Blossom City. The shadow of loss fading in the light of friendship, the pall of regret and betrayal shattering against the foundation of unity and honor.

Good times were coming to Blossom City.

And, Lord, she wanted to be a part of it. Wanted Jason and a chance of a family with him. Wanted to be near her mother and the roots she represented. Wanted a career of her choice rather than one she'd been born into.

Mostly she wanted love. She meant to take Nona's advice and grab at the chance with both hands.

And she knew just the way to get started.

Happy with life, she punched on the radio, twisted the dial until she heard Garth Brooks and sang about taking a chance on life and dancing the dance.

She arrived back in Blossom in time to costume up and open for business by noon. She stood and looked out at the beautiful day, the sky blue and cloud-speckled, a breeze rolling down the midway, offsetting the high temperature.

The scent of popcorn, roasting corn and fried Twinkies floated on that stream of air, with the occasional shift in the breeze sending the earthly aroma of livestock her way.

Comfortable, familiar and slightly out of whack.

Ever since she'd gotten back, something had nagged at her. She couldn't put her finger on just what. But something was off. She'd tried calling Jason to make sure he and Rikki were all right. She'd had to leave a message.

"Lady Pandora, hello. Lady Pandora. We're here for our reading." Two older women waved and shouted to catch her attention.

Cherry smiled. "Mrs. White, Mrs. Davis, good afternoon."

"We're both entered in the apple pie bake-off being judged tonight, and we need you to tell us who's going to win," Mrs. White informed her. "I won last year, Millie the year before."

"As long as it's not the widow Harrison, I don't care. That woman gloats something terrible," Mrs. Davis added.

"Well, come on in ladies, and I'll see what I can do." Cherry ushered the women inside, glancing up and down the midway one last time before she turned and followed them.

She stayed busy for the rest of the afternoon and into the evening. The sun was just going down when she took twenty minutes to snag a hot dog on a stick and a lemonade.

"Junk food?" Jason slid onto the bench seat next to her. A young couple with a toddler sat across from them. "I'm surprised at you."

"Please." She wiped mustard from the corner of her mouth, welcomed his appearance to chase away the nagging feeling that had grown throughout the afternoon. "Fair food is a culinary classic."

"Remind me never to let you feed my child."

"Coward." She allowed her knees to bump into his under cover of the table. "What brings you here?"

"Judging the apple pie bake-off. Annual mayoral duty. Not so bad, except for the political suicide. Lots of good pie in that contest."

"Who won? Mrs. White and Mrs. Davis stopped by earlier. They wanted me to tell them who would win."

"So you should already know who won."

"I consider my sessions to be confidential. Spill the news." Nudging him, she indicated with a lift of her chin he should rise. She followed him up, dumped her trash.

"Mrs. White won." He fell into step as she headed back to her tent. "Not enough cinnamon in Mrs. Davis'."

"Well, at least the widow Harrison didn't win."

His brows lifted. "What do you have against Lydia Harrison?"

"She gloats something terrible." She quoted Mrs. Davis and grinned when Jason's eyes narrowed suspiciously. She decided to keep him guessing. A little mystery never hurt a woman's chances with a man.

"Guess what? I've signed up to take the test to get my GED."

"Hey, that's great." He gave her a quick hug. "I have no doubt you'll ace it."

"Thanks for the vote of confidence. It's your fault, you know. When you said stay last night, it really sounded good. I woke up today and knew I was ready to take a few chances."

He caught her eye, his expression unreadable. "I'm glad."

Not exactly a declaration of love, but she wasn't discouraged. He had a few demons of his own to slay. And she'd seen the way he looked at her last night. He was anything but disinterested.

She decided to change the subject. "Has anything freaky happened today?"

"Freaky how?"

"I don't know. I've just had a weird feeling all day. That something's off, something's going to happen."

For the first time, she realized the twitching had eased when he sat down beside her. Jason grounded her, calmed her in ways nobody else ever had. Not even Nona.

"I haven't heard of anything. I can call Trace."

"Don't bother. Just a feeling I've had."

They strolled the short distance to her tent with shoulders bumping and hands flirting. Even though she'd been close by, she'd locked up. The vandalism attack was too recent to take any chances. As they approached, Cherry saw someone in dark baggy clothes hunched over in front of the tent. The bad feeling returned with a snap.

"Jason, someone's trying to break into my tent."

"I see him, too. But it looks more like he's hanging on than breaking in."

"You're right." In an instant, she knew. "Oh my God. It's Melissa, she's in labor." Cherry rushed forward.

Jason kept pace with her. "Labor? I didn't know she was pregnant."

"She's been hiding it." Cherry reached the slumping figure. "Melissa."

Sweat beaded the girl's pale features. "Lady Pandora. Help. Hurts."

"Melissa, it's okay. I'm here." Cherry put an arm around the girl. Immediately felt pain, confusion, fear. And from another tiny source—the baby—a cry of distress. "I'm going to help you." She turned to Jason. "Call an ambulance." He nodded, started dialing the cell he already had in hand. "And the fair doctor. Get him here now."

"I've already paged Dr. Wilcox. He's on site tonight."

"Good." Cherry gave Jason her keys. "Can you open up so we can get her inside and seated. Out of the middle of the midway?"

The teenager slumped against Cherry. She turned and tucked her shoulder under Melissa's arm to hold her up. "You can sit down in just a minute."

"Can't wait." Melissa's legs gave out on her. In spite of Cherry's added strength, the girl went down, taking Cherry with her.

Melissa whimpered.

"Okay, it's okay." Cherry gritted her teeth; her foot twisted awkwardly under Melissa.

Jason turned away from the tent and bent over the two women. "What can I do to help?" He reached to pull Cherry free.

She shook her head. "I don't think we should move her. Can you lift her shoulders a little so I can get under her back to support her head and shoulders?"

He did as she asked, and Cherry freed her foot. She felt the difference in Melissa as her body relaxed against Cherry.

She put the excited murmurs of the gathering crowd out of her mind to concentrate on helping the laboring girl.

"Melissa, first I want you to breathe. Do it with me, breathe with me." Cherry set up a deep, slow rhythm that she took fast and shallow when a contraction hit.

When the pain passed, Cherry demanded. "How far apart are the pains?"

"Don't know. Fast. My water broke. I didn't know what to do. So I came to you."

"Melissa." Jason crouched beside them, cell ready. "I need to call your father. What's his number?"

Melissa cringed back, turned her head aside. "No. He won't understand."

"Sweetheart," Cherry gently brushed a hand over the girl's tangled hair, "there's no hiding any more."

"No." She shook her head wildly, then tensed and screamed when another contraction hit.

Cherry directed Melissa's breathing, felt the distress in the baby rising. She caught Jason's gaze, hit him with the full weight of her concern. "Where's the doctor? The ambulance?"

"Coming." He turn to someone in the crowd and said, "Find Rev. Tolliver."

"I'm here," a stout voice called. "Right here. Someone said Melissa's sick. Where is she?"

Jason intercepted the man and filled him in on the situation. Rev. Tolliver, in stark black and wearing his collar, barely reached the mayor's shoulder. The reverend's confusion and worry were clear.

As was his outrage that his daughter had sought out the fortune-teller in her time of need.

To his credit, he tried to put that aside. He came to his daughter's side, cast Cherry a scathing look, then dismissed her. "Melissa." He took her hand. "I'm here. Child, why didn't you tell me—"

Melissa moaned and frantically shook her head.

"What is it?" He demanded. "Is this woman hurting you?"

"No." She bit off a scream, panted through a contraction. "I knew you wouldn't understand."

"I understand it was a no-good carny who led you astray. Who shamed you."

"Go away. Go away. I hate you." Melissa turned her head in toward Cherry.

"Reverend, perhaps now isn't the time—" Cherry attempted to intervene.

"Do not," he snapped at Cherry, "tell me how to speak to my daughter."

"Reverend." Jason stood at the man's shoulder.

"I don't want her near my daughter." Tolliver shot to his feet. "She's a bad influence, abetting my child in a life of sin and disobedience."

"She knows what she's doing," Jason said. "She stays until the doctor gets here."

Cherry tried to tune out the arguing. The reverend's posturing, Jason's dedicated neutrality. She murmured softly, reassuringly to Melissa. The girl needed to relax; her tension fought her body's need to expel the child within.

"The doctor is here." A tall man with gray, balding hair and thick glasses pushed through the two men. A medical tech carrying a portable stretcher stopped outside the circle. "I hear a miracle is happening."

Calm and competent, Dr. Wilcox assumed control. He ordered Jason to keep people back while he performed a quick exam. The medical tech used the stretcher to create a privacy screen.

Cherry brought the doctor up to speed, then she took Melissa's hand and concentrated on soothing the frightened, pain-ridden girl.

"She's crowning," Dr. Wilcox declared. "We're going to have to deliver this baby right here."

The news sent a shiver of dread through Cherry. She placed her free hand on Melissa's abdomen over the baby struggling to be born. The life force felt weaker, traumatized but fighting to live. If the doctor attempted a delivery under these conditions, he'd lose Melissa, the baby, or both.

She had to warn him, though with Rev. Tolliver spouting his vitriol mere feet away, she had little chance of convincing anyone of anything.

Still, she must try.

"Dr. Wilcox, please. We must get her to the hospital. The baby is in distress. I have a talent for knowing these things. It's too dangerous."

Jason and the reverend both turned at her words.

"You don't know what you're talking about. You're not a doctor. My daughter's not going anywhere. The doctor said there's no time."

Dr. Wilcox sat back on his heels and ran his gaze over Cherry. He took in her gypsy costume, the banner on her tent advertising Lady Pandora, listened to the crowd chant a protest against the fortune-teller.

Jason said nothing.

Melissa crushed the bones in Cherry's hand. "I want to go to the hospital. I want to do what she says."

"Are you the fortune-teller who predicted Tammy Wright would have a girl?" Dr. Wilcox asked.

"Yes." Cherry's heart sped as she waited for his reaction. "Please believe me, we must get her to the hospital."

"Don't listen to this woman." Rev. Tolliver ranted. "She's a fraud and a menace. She had no right to encourage my daughter to defy me." He rounded on Cherry. "If anything happens to my daughter, I'm suing you for practicing medicine without a license."

"Watch it, Tolliver." Jason stepped between the agitated reverend and Cherry.

Dr. Wilcox ignored them both. "That's good enough for me. Let's get her on the stretcher, meet the ambulance at the gate."

"Thank you, Doctor." The situation was still too critical to feel relief. "We must hurry."

Jason's cell rang. He answered and announced, "The ambulance is here." He spoke back into the phone, "Let them in. We'll meet them on the main drag."

Melissa refused to let go of Cherry, so she assisted Dr. Wilcox, the tech and Jason in lifting her onto the stretcher.

Cherry's tent was on an offshoot of the main drag but food tables and concession stands filled the aisle, preventing the ambulance from accessing it. By the time they reached the main drag, the ambulance was waiting.

The emergency medical technicians quickly transferred Melissa to their stretcher and prepared to lift her into the ambulance. Again, she refused to release her hold on Cherry.

"Come with me," Melissa pleaded.

Cherry looked at the doctor, who nodded.

"No!" Rev. Tolliver immediately protested. He

turned to Jason. "Mayor, stop this woman. I don't want her near my daughter."

Cherry waited to hear Jason defend her, waited to hear him support her. Surely he wouldn't do this to her again. Surely he'd learned to trust her enough to back her against an overemotional, small-minded man.

When he hesitated, she experienced a painful sense of déjà vu.

When he stepped between her and the ambulance, and she saw the regret in his eyes, her heart simply broke in two.

"She's underage," he said. "I have to respect her father's request."

"This isn't about her father. This is about Melissa, who's frightened, in pain and unprepared for what she's going through. She wants my help. She's more child than woman, but she knew how her father would react. He's the one you should be trying to restrain, not me."

"Cherry, don't make this more difficult than it has to be. Just step aside."

"No." Dr. Wilcox climbed from the ambulance where the EMTs had placed Melissa. "The patient is becoming hysterical. Lady Pandora has kept her calm. She needs to come with us. And we need to leave now."

"I don't want her near my daughter!"

The doctor moved forward, towered over the posturing reverend. "I don't really care what you want. I don't know what the history is here. Again, I don't care. My patient comes first."

Rev. Tolliver turned red. "You can't talk to me that way."

"Someone needs to talk sense to you because I'll tell you what I do know. If we don't calm your daughter down, if we don't leave for the hospital now, she may die. It's time for you to climb down off that moral high horse and think of her."

All the color that had rushed into the reverend's face bleached out again. "Die? She's just having a baby."

"She's experiencing difficulties. It's imperative we leave now." Dr. Wilcox didn't wait any longer. He waved Cherry toward the ambulance and then turned to Jason. "Mayor, please escort Rev. Tolliver to the hospital. We'll meet you there."

Without looking at Jason, Cherry put her broken heart aside to climb in next to Melissa, who hugged her belly and cried nonstop. Cherry took her hand. "I'm here Melissa. I'm here for you."

Chapter Eleven

At the hospital, Dr. Wilcox rushed Melissa into an emergency C-section. After the scene at the fair, Cherry preferred not to share a waiting room with Rev. Tolliver or Jason. She asked a nurse if there was somewhere else to wait and the woman directed her to a private room.

In the attached bathroom, she washed up, erasing the more dramatic makeup she used when she worked. She also stripped off the velvet vest and swept her hair up in a clip.

She wished she'd been allowed to go in with Melissa. Then maybe thoughts of Jason and the future they'd never have together wouldn't continue to play and replay in Cherry's mind.

So much for the vision of her, Jason and Rikki as

the ideal family. Obviously, Jason wasn't ready to move on. She saw his need to keep everything on an even keel as a way to control his life.

. If everything stayed the same, there was less chance of losing something. Or someone.

She understood his need for reassurances, for conformity. Just as she'd understood his need to pacify Bitsy Dupres.

Yeah, that was her, an understanding gal. How ironic that she also understood she couldn't live that way. Wouldn't live that way.

Because of him she'd been willing to face her biggest fear. And by God, she still would. She wouldn't allow his small-mindedness to dictate her future.

But it hurt, oh how it hurt, to see him stand between her and respectability.

"Ms. Cooper?" After what seemed like forever, a nurse stuck her blue-capped head in the door.

"Yes." Eager for news, Cherry stepped forward. "How is Melissa Tolliver? The baby?"

"Both doing fine, but it was close. The cord was wrapped around the baby's throat. If you'll come with me, Melissa would like to see you."

"Great." Relief for Melissa, for the baby, made Cherry go limp with exhaustion. Gathering her composure, she followed the woman down two corridors before she stopped and opened a door, standing aside for Cherry to enter.

The homey room held a sofa, a chair and a TV, as

well as the hospital bed and a wheeled, clear plastic, infant bed.

The sight of Rev. Tolliver next to Melissa's bed gave Cherry pause.

"Ms. Cooper, please come in," the reverend said.

She hiked her chin and walked to the other side of the bed. Melissa looked drawn and exhausted. But her hair had been brushed and clipped back to reveal pretty blue eyes and plump features stamped with pride and awe as she gazed at her baby.

"Isn't she beautiful?" Melissa asked not taking her eyes off the miracle in her arms.

"Gorgeous." And she was, all pink and soft and tiny. Just as a baby should be. "You did a good job."

"No, I didn't. She wouldn't be here if not for you. But I promise to do better from now on." Melissa traced the fine dark eyebrows causing the little forehead to crinkle in a frown. "Daddy's going to help me. You were right about that, too."

"I owe you an apology, Ms. Cooper." Rev. Tolliver stated stiffly. "Melissa told me how you encouraged her to confide her condition to me. My behavior at the fair was unconscionable. I was shocked and frantic with worry. I didn't handle it well. I'm sorry."

Cherry nodded, accepting the apology, accepting the difficulty with which it was given. "I'm glad all ended well."

"Dr. Wilcox said we may have lost the baby if he'd delivered at the fairgrounds."

"I said we would have lost both Melissa and the

baby if I delivered at the fairgrounds," Dr. Wilcox interjected, joining Cherry at the bedside and looking down on mother and child. "You're a very lucky young lady. And you, Ms. Cooper, are very insightful. The cord had wrapped around the baby's neck. If we'd continued, I believe the placenta would have ruptured. You saved the day."

"You were willing to listen. Thank you, Doctor."

He winked at Melissa. "Seems we need a name for the new Miss Tolliver."

Melissa glanced up at Cherry, her gaze half-shy, half-awed. "I'd like to name her after Lady Pandora."

"Oh, well." Flustered, Cherry blushed with pleasure. "I'm honored, but surely you'd prefer a family name."

"You saved her, I want her to have your name," Melissa said, all earnestness. "Please."

"All right, but Lady Pandora's a stage name. My real name is Blossom Ann Cooper."

"Blossom? Really? That's funny, huh?" Melissa yawned. "That you have the same name as our city? I like Ann. I'll call her Annie. My little…Annie." Melissa slipped into sleep.

"Annie Tolliver. I'll inform the nurse staff." Dr. Wilcox turned to go. "Well done, Ms. Cooper. Come see me if you ever need a job."

Cherry left father to look after daughter and granddaughter and headed out. At the nurses' station, she asked for directions to a public phone.

The nurse smiled. "Hey, you're the hero of the

hour around here." She turned a phone around to face Cherry. "Just dial nine first to get an outside line."

"Thanks." Cherry called Carlo, told him she needed a ride home from the hospital. He already knew what had happened at the fairgrounds. She filled him in on the rest. He promised to have someone pick her up at the front doors.

Since she came through the emergency entrance, she asked the nurse for directions, then followed them toward the elevators.

Cherry had herself a namesake. Pretty amazing. At least Melissa had a happy ending today. She gave birth to a healthy baby girl and reconciled with her father. Now that was cool.

Thank God for Dr. Wilcox.

Well done, he'd said. And offered her a job. Too bad she no longer had a reason to stay. No, that wasn't right. Too bad she no longer had a desire to stay. The last thing she wanted was the chance of running into Jason.

"Cherry." Jason suddenly stepped into her path. "I've been waiting for you."

His hair stood on end, his collar askew, and he looked more haggard than she'd ever seen him. Clearly he'd found the wait painful.

A small vindictive part of her was glad. "You shouldn't have."

He blocked her when she tried to side step around him. Taking her elbow, he pulled her into the vacant waiting room he'd appeared from. An empty nonde-

script room with plenty of chairs, plenty of maga-
zines and a muted TV.

"I know you're hurt. That I hurt you." He reached
for her to pull her close, to offer comfort, but he
never got his hands on her.

She backed away, crossed her arms over her
chest, and met his remorseful gaze with a steely one
of her own.

"Yeah, you did."

"He's her father. You know I had no choice but to
uphold his rights."

"I know it was easier."

"That's not true." He raked a hand through his hair
doing more damage to the spiked ends. "I never
wanted to cause you pain."

"But you did, because it allowed you to be in control, made you look good in front of the CMB and
all the good citizens of Blossom gathered around."

"I was thinking of you." He bit off a curse when
she sidestepped him again. His tone turned hard. "Do
you know what the good citizens of Blossom would
do to you if anything had happened to Melissa while
in your care?"

Cherry blinked at his vehemence. Maybe more
thought had gone into his decision than she'd given
him credit for. "She was in the doctor's care by then."

"It wouldn't have mattered. You would have been
the scapegoat if anything went wrong."

She closed in on herself. Giving him a wide berth,
she successfully rounded him to reach the entrance

to the room. "The people of Blossom can't hurt me. It doesn't matter what they do, what they think, because they don't really know me. They're judging a character I play, not the person I am."

"Cherry," Jason pleaded. "It's not that simple."

"I know you think if you keep everything contained you can maintain control, but that's an illusion, Jason. Doing nothing doesn't prevent you from doing the wrong thing. It just keeps you from moving forward."

She hugged herself, trying to keep in the emotion.

"I thought you were different. I thought you knew me, knew I would never do anything to endanger a child's life. I guess I thought wrong." Tears rose to clog her throat, threatened to overflow down her cheeks. She needed to get out of there before she humiliated herself in front of him. "Please don't come around me again."

She dodged out the door, made it all the way to the elevator and inside before the first tears escaped.

Jason slid onto a stool in The Alibi, a ramshackle bar on the outskirts of town across the road from the fairgrounds. Egg-carton insulation and chicken-wire repairs aside, The Alibi rated high as a local honky-tonk.

Business was brisk with out-of-towners enjoying the benefits of a wet county. Jason sat for a couple of minutes before Grady, the owner and bartender, spotted him and brought over a beer.

He sulked over his mug of brew, replaying and rethinking the events of the day, wondering how he could have done anything differently.

Cherry clearly thought he could have handled events better. Considering he'd managed to side with the CMB against her yet again, he hardly blamed her. After that fine display, she'd probably never believe he loved her.

Loved? His head went back as if he'd taken one on the chin.

Where did that come from?

Was it true?

Did he love Cherry?

He waited for the sorrow and betrayal of Diane to rush forward, to overwhelm him with guilt. When it didn't, when fear of losing Cherry obliterated all other thoughts, he remembered what she'd said about honoring a first love by being able to find love and happiness again.

Someone slapped his back, then squeezed in next to him amidst the crush of people at the bar. "Hey, buddy. I hear all hell broke loose at the fair today."

Jason toasted his old friend Blake Gray Feather. "That about describes it."

"Tough." The champion rodeo star tipped back his dark head, sipped his bear. "I heard the girl is all right. And the baby. So it didn't all turn out bad."

"No," Jason confirmed. "Just my life."

"Ah, trouble with the beautiful Lady Pandora?"

Jason eyed his friend with suspicion. "What makes you say that?"

"Come on." Blake nudged Jason's shoulder. "Everyone knows you two are an item."

"Define everyone."

"Townspeople. Cowboys. Carnies. Everyone. It's the talk of the fair."

Jason groaned. "Great. My life on parade."

"Nothing new in that," Blake said, tossing back a handful of peanuts. "You're mayor aren't you?"

"Which hasn't interfered with my private life until now."

"Cindy," Blake mentioned his fiancée and Jason's neighbor, "tells me you haven't had a private life until now. Everyone's happy for you. Well, except for the CMB folks. What's with them, anyway?"

Jason waved a dismissive hand. "Don't get me started. I have to keep reminding myself they mean well."

"Then what's standing between you and Cherry?"

"Apparently, my inability to move beyond my comfort zone."

"Say what?"

"According to her, I keep everything contained in order to maintain control, but it's all an illusion that prevents me from moving forward."

"Sounds deep. What do you think it means?"

"I don't know. I've always been someone to take charge, be in control. Since I lost Diane, it's gotten worse, become almost a compulsion."

"Well, buddy, I don't know what to tell you, except maybe it's time you stepped outside that nice tidy box. With my background, I was afraid I had nothing to offer Cindy. She convinced me I was wrong and I've never been happier. And surprise, nobody thinks it's strange we're a couple."

Jason spun on his stool to face his friend. "Because there's nothing strange about it. You grew up here. This is your home. You guys make a great couple."

Blake bumped beers with Jason. "She's the best thing to ever happen to me. But my point is this isn't Cherry's world. She may feel she has nothing to offer you. Your siding with the CMB would confirm that, in her opinion."

Hearing his fears put into words made Jason all the more sure they were true. Never mind she was the brightest, most compassionate, funniest woman he'd ever met. He knew she suffered from insecurities. Hadn't a fear of falling short in his world kept her from pursuing a career as a midwife? She'd told him of her fear, yet he hadn't really listened.

"So how do I convince her we belong together?"

"Tell her you love her. And here's the important part." Blake clasped Jason's shoulder as if imparting something of the utmost significance. "Don't take no for an answer. I almost lost Cindy because I didn't think love was enough."

"Got it. Don't take no for an answer."

The next evening, Cherry locked up her tent and threaded her way through the midway to the Ferris wheel. Carlo had called to say he needed her help.

She wondered exactly how she'd be able to help him, but it didn't really matter. He'd helped her plenty of times, and she'd been ready for a break, so off to the Ferris wheel she went.

Once she finished with Carlo, she'd swing by her trailer for dinner. Or maybe not. That would require she spend time with her own thoughts. Maybe the twins would like to get something to eat.

A light breeze teased the air, plastering her skirt to her body, then causing it to billow. The setting sun painted the sky pink and orange. The huge Ferris wheel stood still, silhouetted against the beauty of the Texas skyline. Carlo crouched next to the controls.

"Hey," she greeted him. "What's up?"

He stood up, wiping his hands on a rag. "Not the Ferris wheel, unfortunately. I appreciate your help. I'm spread thin tonight."

"No problem. What do you need me to do?"

"Can you go up on the platform and watch the clearance as the cars go by?"

"Sure." Sounded simple enough. Cherry walked around and climbed up the stairs of the platform. An empty car, bar raised sat as if waiting for the next customers to climb aboard. "Ready," she called so Carlo would know she was in position.

"Me, too," Jason said looming up behind Cherry. He clasped her around the waist and with easy strength lifted her into the waiting car. He pulled the bar down over their laps. "Ready," he called.

The big wheel began to move, lifting them backward into the clear evening sky.

"What are you doing?" she demanded, grabbing the bar as they rose higher. "I thought we agreed you were going to stay away."

"No, you told me to stay away. But I can't do it, Cherry." He set his hand over hers on the bar. "You mean too much to me. I can't let you go."

"Jason, you're just dragging out the inevitable." She tried to pull away, but he held firm.

The car reached the top and the big wheel stopped. The car rocked gently, Blossom City in all its dusk-lit glory spread out below them. The bright lights of the carnival blended into a festive rainbow.

Distracted by Jason, Cherry hadn't immediately noted Carlo's participation in this little escapade. No way Jason succeeded in shanghaiing her without her friend's help. She wouldn't forget it later. The man would pay.

"Jason..." What could she say that hadn't already been said. She'd rehashed the events and possibilities in her mind until her head ached and her heart bled. Always she came to the same conclusion. As long as Jason fixated on the past instead of the present, they stood no chance of a future together.

Not that he'd ever shown any indication of wanting a future with her.

"Cherry." He lifted her hand from the bar, brought it to his mouth. He pressed a warm kiss in the very center before bringing her hand to his chest and pressing it against his heart.

Under her trembling fingers and his white shirt, she felt the rapid beat of his heart. How interesting. He wasn't as calm as he appeared.

He lifted her chin, causing her gaze to rise from the sight of his hand resting over hers to meet his gray-blue eyes.

"First, I want to apologize for yesterday. Whatever my motives, I hurt you. For that I'm sorry."

Cherry sighed. "I know it wasn't intentional. Or done lightly. I could see how torn you were. But that doesn't change the fact that in a choice between me and the town, the town always wins. It's best for both of us if we stay away from each other. Then no one has to choose."

"Too late. I choose you. Yesterday I knew you'd be hurt, that there wasn't time to explain, especially with Rev. Tolliver standing right there. But I wasn't prepared for how much the look of shock and betrayal on your face would tear me apart. Then I couldn't find you and when I did, you wouldn't talk to me."

"I saw no reason to keep repeating history. Talking just makes it hurt more. Can't we just agree to be friends and leave it at that?"

"I want to be your friend, yes. But that's not enough. I want to be your lover, your husband, the love of your life."

"Jason." Shock and disbelief had her shaking her head. "You don't know what you're saying."

"I do. And that's what I hope you'll be saying—
I do."

Cherry shook her head. "We have so many things
working against us."

He squeezed her fingers. "You're the bravest
woman I know. You were willing to face your fears
for me. It's time I faced mine for you. There's nothing we can't do together."

"It's not that simple," she protested.

"I don't expect it to be simple." He fingered her hair,
twirled a silky corkscrew around his index finger. "I do
expect it to be worth it. Can you see my future, Cherry?
You can't, can you? Because you can't see your own
future. Doesn't that prove we're meant to be together?"

Uncertainty warred with hope. "I don't know. I
just don't know."

"Hello," a tiny voice came over a loud speaker.
"Did she say yes yet?"

Cherry turned a startled look on Jason. "Is that
Rikki?"

He grinned. "Yeah, and a few others I invited to
witness the joyous occasion. It is going to be joyous,
right?"

Cherry leaned past him to look over the side of the
car. She blinked as a spotlight aimed at them blinded
her. Finally, she looked beyond the light. A whole
crowd of people stared up from below. Cindy Tucker
and her beau, Blake Gray Feather stood next to Sheriff Trace McCabe. Carlo and Dutch and Buster chatted with the twins, still dressed in their belly-dancing

costumes. And surprise, surprise, Mrs. White and Mrs. Davis stood elbow to elbow with Minnie Dressler. All three women waved.

And sure enough, there was Hannah with Rikki, and, oh my God, Nona. Rikki sat in Nona's lap in a wheelchair. As Cherry's heart swelled to overflowing, Rikki put the megaphone to her mouth.

"Cherry, will you be my mommy?" Her little voice came through loud and clear.

Cherry sat back with enough thump to rock the car.

"Easy." He wrapped an arm around her shoulders to steady her.

"You brought Nona here." Tears blurred her vision. She knuckled away the wetness. "I can't believe you brought Nona here."

"Hey." He swiped a thumb over her cheek. "It's supposed to make you happy. I want this to be a special moment for you. My family's here for me. I wanted your family to be here for you. That meant Nona. We had to promise to have her back by tomorrow evening. She said to tell you this was a move worthy of Prince Charming."

"She's right." Cherry laughed. "Thank you." Threading her fingers into his dark hair, she pulled him close, kissed him softly. "You're so sweet."

He kissed her back, taking it deeper, drawing out the heat. "I love you."

She smiled against his lips. "You invited Minnie Dressler? CMB member, biggest-gossip-in-town Minnie Dressler?"

"Yeah." He kissed the corner of her mouth, nibbled his way to her ear. "So I'm really hoping you're going to say yes. Will you marry me, Cherry Blossom Cooper? Will you be my wife, and Rikki's mother? Tell me you'll stay in Blossom and make it your home."

"Yes." Love and hope and happiness swelled up, broke out in a burst of words peppered by kisses. "I love you. So much. The answer is yes. Yes. Yes. And yes." She sat back look earnestly into his eyes. "You're sure?"

"Baby, the first time I saw you I thought trouble had come to town on a Harley. Well, you wrote trouble all over my heart. The best kind of trouble, the kind that made me think and feel. Made me laugh and worry. You brought me to life again. And yes, I'm sure I want to live that life with you."

"The first time I touched you I knew I'd found my soul mate. I can't see our future, so I can't say we'll live happily ever after, but I promise to love you forever."

"That's good enough for me." He leaned in for another kiss, then raised his arm to signal Carlo. A moment later, the car surged into movement. As the crowd of well wishers came into view, Jason raised a triumphant fist in the air. "She said yes."

Everyone broke into applause, accompanied by a few wolf whistles. That would be the twins.

Cherry laughed in delight. When they reached bottom, Carlo plunked a giggling Rikki between Cherry and Jason.

"How about a free ride for the happy family?" Carlo stepped back and twisted a finger in the air. A moment later, the ride started in again.

Rikki shrieked in excited enchantment. Cherry rested her head on Jason's shoulder and let the joy overtake her. As Blossom came into view again, she smiled softly. The town still had some healing to do, but she had a really good feeling about the city's future.

Good times were coming to Blossom.

* * * * *

Don't miss the continuation of
BLOSSOM COUNTY FAIR
Where love blooms true!
THE SHERIFF WINS A WIFE
By Jill Limber
Silhouette Romance #1784
September 2005
HER GYPSY PRINCE
By Crystal Green
Silhouette Romance #1789
October 2005

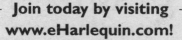

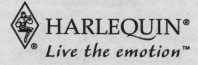

If you enjoyed what you just read,
then we've got an offer you can't resist!

Take 2 bestselling
love stories FREE!
Plus get a FREE surprise gift!

SILHOUETTE *Romance* ®

COMING NEXT MONTH

#1782 THE TEXAN'S TINY DILEMMA—
Judy Christenberry
Lone Star Brides

Theresa Tyler's hidden pregnancy wouldn't prove half as
difficult as interpreting the father's response. Sure, she burned
for James Schofield, but she wanted to be chosen by *his* heart, not
by his upright nature. Were his actions only dutiful gestures, or
did something lurk beneath them? If only she could trust what *her*
heart was telling her, and not her head!

#1783 PRINCE BABY—Susan Meier
Bryant Baby Bonanza

Marrying Seth Bryant only two weeks after meeting him was
Princess Lucy Santos's most spontaneous moment. But when Lucy
learned she was pregnant with Seth's son—her country's future
king—she found herself caught up in a web of royal desires and
private concerns. Would these threats blind the young couple to their
original desires—or would love reign triumphant?

#1784 THE SHERIFF WINS A WIFE—Jill Limber
Blossom County Fair

When Jennifer Williams left Blossom County for the lure of big city
life, Trace McCabe was crushed by the knowledge that he'd never
see the love-of-his-life again. But eight years later, Jenn was back
in Blossom—temporarily—to help her pregnant sister, and Trace
vowed to do whatever it took to win the heart of his first love....

#1785 ONCE UPON A KING—Holly Jacobs
Perry Square: The Royal Invasion!

Three months ago Cara Phillips shared a night with a gorgeous
mystery man only to find him gone when she awoke. Imagine her
surprise when she shows up to serve as bridesmaid at a wedding and
learns he's not only her friend's brother but a prince to boot! But
will the prince ride off into the sunset once he learns Cara's most
closely guarded secret—or can this fairy tale have a happy ending
after all?

SRCNM0805